Bittersweet Summer

by Anne Warren Smith

Anne Warren Smith

Albert Whitman & Company
Chicago, Illinois

Also by Anne Warren Smith:

Turkey Monster Thanksgiving

Tails of Spring Break

Library of Congress Cataloging-in-Publication data
Smith, Anne Warren.
Bittersweet Summer /by Anne Warren Smith
p. cm.

Summary: Nine-year-old Katie and her four-year-old brother, Tyler, have an emotional summer during which their father considers moving them to Portland and they are surprised by a visit with their mother, a country singer.

ISBN 978-0-8075-0763-6 (hardcover)
[1. Family life—Oregon—Fiction. 2. Single-parent families—Fiction.
3. Moving, Household—Fiction. 4. Mothers and sons—Fiction.
5. Mothers and daughters—Fiction. 6. Oregon—Fiction.] I. Title.
PZ7.S6427 Bit 2012 [Fic]—dc22 2011008570

Published in 2012 by Albert Whitman & Company.

Printed in the United States of America.

10 9 8 7 6 5 4 3 2 1 LB 16 15 14 13 12 11

Designed by Lindaanne Donohoe

For more information about Albert Whitman & Company, visit our website at www.albertwhitman.com.

For Jerry

Contents

Chapter 1

The Last Day of Fourth Grade

The Fourth Grade room was unusually quiet as the line of sad kids shuffled forward. We were saying good-bye to Ms. Morgan.

I swallowed back my tears and tasted end-of-school fruit punch and end-of-school lemon cupcakes. My throat hurt and my stomach gurgled as I got into the good-bye line.

Claire Plummer stepped in next to me. "She's the most beautiful teacher I ever had," she said in a dreary, woeful voice as she tugged at her blond curls. Claire hoped that tugging would make her hair longer, but she would never have a long, beautiful ponytail like Ms. Morgan's. Besides, Ms. Morgan's hair was brown.

"Fifth grade will be fun," Ms. Morgan said to Tiffany who was four people ahead of us. "You'll see."

"I already hate fifth grade," I said to my best friend, Sierra, who stood on the other side of me. She and Claire nodded. We all sighed.

Ms. Morgan hugged Doug Backer and then Ethan Murphy and then Alex Ramirez.

"How can she stand hugging Alex in that old, ratty shirt?" Claire whispered.

"It doesn't smell," Sierra said. All at once, her face turned red. "He sat in front of me," she added. "I sniffed it once."

We giggled.

Maybe, I thought, Alex loved that flannel shirt the way I loved my orange hooded sweatshirt. Of course, my sweatshirt didn't hang down to my knees. And I didn't wear it to school every day.

"Hi, Claire," Ms. Morgan said as Claire stepped forward. "You and your dad made this a special year for me."

"It was our pleasure," Claire's dad called from the back of the room. He had been the room father all year. Now, he was doing his last chores: gathering up paper napkins and paper cups from the party. He had made the lemon cupcakes. I swallowed again as Ms. Morgan hugged Claire.

Claire had been the perfect student. I had not. Three times, I had over-watered the sunflower. Three times, muddy water had flooded the windowsills.

Sierra got the next hug. "I loved seeing your rock collection," Ms. Morgan said to her. "You might grow up to be a scientist."

"Thanks for being my teacher," Sierra said.

As I stepped forward, I wondered if Ms. Morgan was secretly glad I was going on to fifth grade. I had done so many terrible things. When I added extra lines to my part in the class play, everybody forgot what they were supposed to do next. When I bumped into the big shamrock poster on St. Patrick's Day, it knocked everything off Ms. Morgan's desk. Her purse, three jars of pencils, a box of filing cards, her big dictionary.

"Good-bye," I said and started to leave. But she took both my hands and pulled me close.

"Katie," she said. "You were my most . . ." She stopped to think. "...my most enthusiastic student."

"Thanks," I mumbled.

"You get excited about things. That's a wonderful way to be." She smiled her beautiful smile, and her green eyes sparkled. "I bet you will have adventures this summer."

"I might," I answered, happy that she was acting like she really liked me. I breathed deep to keep her vanilla-pudding smell with me as long as possible.

Sierra tugged on my arm. "My mom is probably waiting," she said.

I ran to gather up my artwork. We couldn't put it off any longer.

Fourth grade was over, and my summer adventures were about to begin.

Chapter 2

Goodbye, Best Friend

We burst out the school door into June sunshine and stood blinking.

Sierra looked at the row of cars in front of school. "She's not even here." She plopped herself down on the top step. "She told me to be ready to go the minute school ended. So where is she?"

"I wish you weren't leaving today," I said. I squinched my eyes to hold back the tears. This sad day was getting worse and worse.

"Where are you going?" Claire asked Sierra.

"Seattle," Sierra answered. "To see my grandma."

"For two weeks," I added. Sierra and I exchanged a sad look.

Sierra patted the step beside her, and I sat down, too. We leaned against each other. We had been best friends forever. Since day care.

I bent over to tie my shoe. "You'll probably have lots of fun in Seattle."

She nodded. "My dad says my grandma is sometimes too full of fun. We never know what she'll think up next."

"My grandma is old," Claire said, tugging on her hair again. "She's always going off to play bridge with her old friends. Her house smells like dust."

"My grandma's house smells like artist's paints," Sierra said. "I might help her get her paintings ready for the galleries." She grabbed my arm and tucked it under hers. "But I would rather be here."

Claire looked at her silver-and-blue wristwatch. "We should start walking, Katie."

"Not until Sierra's mom comes." I squinted up at Claire, who was standing between us and the blinding sun. "How come your dad can't drive us home today? He's right here."

"He has an appointment," she said. "He told me we should walk."

Since Claire's house was across the street from my house, our dads made us walk together. They said pairs were safer. They also expected us to be friends since we both didn't have mothers at home.

Sometimes, Claire and I were friends. Sometimes, we were not.

Sierra patted the step on the other side of her. "Sit down, Claire. My mom will be here in a minute."

Claire wrinkled her nose. "Those steps are filthy. How can you stand it?"

Sierra and I rolled our eyes at each other as Claire paced up and down the sidewalk, shading her eyes and looking for Sierra's mom.

"I'm going to be stuck with Claire," I told Sierra, "for two weeks."

"Let's plan something fun for when I get back," Sierra said. "Like, let's go to the pool."

"Starting tomorrow, I'll be very busy," Claire said as she stood in front of us again. "There's ballet and piano. And—." She stopped and looked sideways at Sierra and me. "—an important project."

"What important project?" I asked.

"I can't tell you," she said. She set her blue book bag down and looked inside it. "I hope my sunglasses are in here."

Suddenly a wonderful idea flew into my mind. I grabbed Sierra's arm. "I know a great thing to do. This summer, once you're back, let's ride our bikes to each other's houses." I jiggled up and down on the step, imagining the joy of it. Whooshing down Benson Street. Zooming into Sierra's driveway.

Sierra's eyes shone at me. "That will be so cool. We'll see each other every day."

"Your parents will never let you bike so far," Claire said. She pulled out a pair of large sunglasses, blue of course, and looked through them at the sky. "Dusty," she said, and began fishing into her bag again.

"It's only eight blocks from my house to yours," Sierra said. "Only one busy street to cross." She turned to me. "You work on your dad, and I'll work on my mom. We'll get them to say yes."

A horn honked just then, and Sierra's mom leaned out of their car. "Sorry I'm late," she called. "We have to get on the road."

Sierra gathered her papers together and stood up. "See you, Katie," she said. "You, too, Claire."

I hugged her good-bye. Once again, I swallowed my tears.

She climbed into her car and waved at us again before Mrs. Dymond drove away.

"At last we can go." Claire put on her blue sunglasses and checked how they looked in a little mirror.

As we started across the playground, I turned to look back at the school. No more Ms. Morgan. No best friend for two weeks. The sour taste of lemon cupcakes came back into my mouth. This summer vacation was starting out awful.

Chapter 3

Claire's Summer Project

Claire and I crossed the playground and turned toward home.

"I can't believe Ms. Morgan won't be my teacher anymore," Claire said. "I already miss her so much."

I kicked a stone off the sidewalk and watched it clatter into the street. "I wonder what she does all summer when there's no school."

"She's lonely," Claire said, stopping to pull up her blue socks. Claire had more blue clothes than anyone else in school. "Her mom and dad and aunts and uncles live in Minnesota."

"She might not know what to do when it's vacation." I kicked at another stone and stubbed my toe.

"She's going to miss writing on the board," Claire said.

"She told the class she might see us at the library," I said. "She wants to read a lot this summer."

"I forgot! I was going to find out where she lives!" Claire's face suddenly got a secret look.

"Why?"

"So I can start my summer project." Claire looked away from me. "I thought I could visit her. I'll take her one of my beautiful beaded bracelets."

A sweaty jogger huffed past us as we crossed onto our street. If I took Ms. Morgan a present, what would I take? She liked the pictures I drew. Lately, I was drawing birds. "Your summer project is making a bracelet?"

Claire shook her head and walked faster. "It's lots bigger than that."

"I've got projects, too," I said, even though I couldn't think of any. We walked along in silence. We were almost home.

"All right," she said, slowing down. "My project is about Ms. Morgan."

I walked backward so I could see Claire's face. "What about her?"

"I told my dad that he should marry her," she said. "He says she's pretty, but they're not in love. I have to make them fall in love."

I screeched to a halt, and Claire almost bumped into me. Mr. Plummer marry Ms. Morgan? If anybody married Ms. Morgan, it should be my dad. Not Claire's.

"She loves me already." Claire flung her arms out and began to walk like a model. "She smiles at me all the time."

"She smiles at everybody," I answered. "She even smiles at Alex Ramirez." She even smiles at me, I thought.

"Alex Ramirez doesn't count," Claire said. "In that old shirt."

"He loves that shirt," I said. "He's okay."

"I bet his mother never lets him into her store looking like that," Claire said.

"What store?"

"The wonderful bride store! On Ninth Street!" Claire clasped her hands together and whirled around. "I can just see Ms. Morgan getting married to my father and me. I will wear something long and shiny from that store."

"She would like my dad better," I said. I wondered if she would.

"She can't like your dad," Claire said. "Your mother wouldn't let her."

"My mother wouldn't care." Or would she? I didn't know that, either.

"My father is very handsome," Claire continued. "And look at my house. It's the nicest one on the block."

Claire's house sparkled white in the sunshine. Her big porch was lined with pots of yellow pansies. Across the street, at my house, my five-year-old brother's toys spilled off the porch and down the walk.

"Now that fourth grade is over," Claire said, "Ms. Morgan is totally free to fall in love with my father. I think there's a rule about room fathers, but after today, he's not the room father any more."

"That's ridiculous," I said.

"You still have a mother," Claire said. She pushed up her blue sunglasses and stared at me. "Mine is gone forever."

It was true that Claire's mother was gone forever. Her mother had died in an accident when we were in second grade. "My parents are seriously divorced," I told her. "Mom travels all the time, doing her concerts."

"She'll come back," Claire said, dropping her glasses back onto her nose, "when she's tired of singing."

"She loves singing. She'll never get tired of it."

"Ms. Morgan is my project, and you can't have her, Katie." Claire looked both ways, even though there was hardly ever traffic on our street, and crossed to the other side.

I climbed over Tyler's pedal car to get to the porch. I hadn't dreamed about Mom being back home in months and months. Even with no mother at home, things were fine the way they were—with Dad and my little brother Tyler and me.

I was pretty sure about that.

Chapter 4

Big Trouble

"I'm home," I called as I stepped into my house.

Tyler came running down the hall to meet me. His red hair bounced up and down. "Katie," he hollered, "it's summer vacation. No more day care."

I dropped my stack of artwork into a chair and pulled off my shoes.

"We have to start playing." He tugged me into the living room.

I stopped at the door. The living room didn't look like our living room. "What's going on in here?"

"Mother-mouse caves." Tyler ran around the room waving his arms. "Here. And here. And here!"

He was pointing at shoes and boots and slippers. He had tucked them into every place a shoe or a boot or a slipper might tuck.

"Mouse caves?" My old blue tennis shoe lay on its side on the coffee table. Something white was stuffed into it.

"MOTHER-mouse caves," he whispered. He reached into my tennis shoe and pulled out a tissue ball. "This is Applepie," he said. "She's waiting to have her babies." He shook the mouse-ball next to his ear and listened. "Any time now," he said.

I peered at the tissue ball, half expecting to see it turn into a real mouse and jump out of Tyler's hand. He tucked the mouse back and pulled another white mouse from a red boot that stood in the bookcase.

"There are seventy-thirteen mother mouses here," he said. "Almost ready to have little mouse babies. We will be very busy."

"Does Dad know you took all our shoes? And that you're using up all the toilet paper?"

"Not yet." Tyler tugged up his shorts and grinned at me. "He's on the phone."

I picked up my artwork. "I have pictures," I said. "I hope these mice like bird drawings." I ran around the room, tucking my drawings next to shoes and into the chairs.

"That's good, Katie." Tyler put his hand on my arm and looked up at me with his round blue eyes. "When it's time for the babies, I'm going to need lots more toilet paper."

"Don't look at me," I said. "I hope you left one roll for the people."

"Hi, Katie," Dad's voice said, making me jump. "It's good you're home. I'm going to have to run to the store. We're almost out of toilet paper."

He stopped then, staring into the living room.

"Tyler made mouse caves," I said. "They're pretty cute, Dad."

"MOTHER-mouse caves," Tyler said.

"I can't believe it," Dad said. "One hour ago, I had this room looking great."

Tyler nodded and stood up straighter.

"Whoa," Dad said. "We've got to get on the same track here. This house has to be spruced up."

"Spruced up? What's that?" Tyler asked.

"Cleaned up. I'm going to need you kids to help me make the house look good."

I squinted at him. That didn't sound like Dad. Usually, he didn't care one bit how the house looked. Usually, he liked things like mouse caves.

But Dad's face looked different today. Worried, maybe. All at once, that sour taste came back into my mouth. I sat down on the floor next to a mouse cave and looked up at him. "What's going on?"

Chapter 5

Bad News from Dad

"I'm going to make a cup of coffee," Dad said, "and then I'll come back and tell you what's going on." He started toward the kitchen and then turned. "When I come back in here, I want this room looking good."

"But," I said, "Tyler made all the . . ."

A frown crossed Dad's face. "I see your pictures all around. I think both of you can work on this."

Dad hardly ever yelled at us. Even when he had too much work from Mr. Flagstaff. Even when I accidently invited people to a Thanksgiving dinner that was supposed to be just for us.

He was waiting. That frown was still there.

I got to my feet.

Dad went toward the kitchen.

"My beautiful mother-mouse caves," Tyler wailed.

"I have a great idea," I said. "Let's make a hotel cave. We'll make it behind the couch."

It took a while, but when we finished the room looked almost normal. All our shoes were piled on their sides behind the couch, little ones on top of big ones. "That's a lot of mother mice," I whispered.

Tyler tucked the last mouse into place and looked around the room. "We are spruced up."

"Our living room looks like Claire's house."

"At Claire's house," Tyler said, "nobody can build anything!"

"Maybe somebody important is coming to see us." I sat cross-legged on the floor and stacked my pictures together.

"Maybe Mr. Friend is coming," Tyler said. "When he came for Thanksgiving dinner, he played trucks with me. We builded bridges all over this room."

"Mr. Flagstaff is in Germany," I told him. "He's not coming." Mr. Flagstaff was an engineer, and Dad worked for him, writing thick reports. He said it was a great job because he could work here at home.

The smell of coffee came first, and then Dad walked in. "Much better," he said, looking around. He straightened the cushions on the couch.

Straightening cushions! That's what Claire's dad is always doing, I thought. I squinted my eyes again at Dad. Something was definitely wrong with him.

He sat down on the couch and took a long sniff of coffee. That was normal. Dad loved sniffing coffee as much as he loved drinking it.

"This week," he said, "I had to make some phone calls for Mr. Flagstaff because he's in Germany. I found out that he's no longer consulting for some of the big companies." Dad stared into his coffee mug. "I'm afraid he's getting ready to retire. If he does, pretty soon there won't be any work for me."

"Good." I set my pictures on the coffee table. "You'll have time to play with us."

He shook his head at me. "I need to be working, Pumpkin. That's how I make money for us to buy groceries."

"Like toilet paper," Tyler said, nodding at me.

"I'm going to need your help," Dad said. "We need to make some big decisions here."

I sat up straight. I liked it when Dad needed my help.

He continued. "A wonderful company in Portland may offer me a job."

Tyler and I stared at him.

"If I get a job in Portland, we'll have to live there."

"Live in Portland?" I felt air whoosh out of me. "We can't do that!"

"It's about two hours away," Dad said. "Too far for me to drive every day."

Tyler kicked his feet against the couch and frowned.

"If we move," Dad said, "we'll need to sell this house. A real estate person is coming tomorrow to talk about that." He sighed. "All the jobs are in Portland."

I looked around our living room, almost all spruced up now. I remembered Tyler sitting on this rug, racing trucks with Mr. Flagstaff. I remembered me reading books to Tyler in the big, green chair. Out the front window, there was Claire's house. I was used to looking out that window at Claire's house.

Right then, I remembered Claire's plans for Ms. Morgan. Could she make it happen? I wondered. Would Ms. Morgan be her new mother? Claire's life would be wonderful. And mine? I rubbed a sad place in my stomach.

"Whatever happens, we'll be fine," Dad said. He pulled both of us into his lap. "You kids are not to worry. We'll still be the three of us. We're still a family no matter where we live."

I listened to Dad's heart beating next to my ear. It wasn't helping me feel better.

Dad shifted us around so he could see our faces. "Now, tell me about the last day of school, Katie. Did you have a party?"

I blew a big sigh out of my mouth.

"The food made me sick," I said. "And Sierra is gone for two weeks. And Claire has a really stupid summer project."

Tears suddenly came into my eyes, and I blinked hard to make them go away. "And now, we might have to move." More tears ran down my cheeks. "It's hardly started, and I hate this summer vacation!"

Chapter 6

Claire's Project: The First Step

We sat in the spruced-up living room while I tried to stop crying. Then the phone rang.

Dad lifted Tyler and me off his lap and ran to his office.

A moment later, he stuck his head in the door. "It's Claire," he said. "Before you talk to her, I want to tell you this moving thing is a secret. Please don't tell Claire we might be moving."

I looked at Tyler. Dad looked at Tyler, too. We both knew Tyler couldn't keep a secret longer than one minute.

"Never mind," Dad said.

I rubbed tears from my cheeks as I walked to his office. The idea that we might move made my feet stumble. My sadness about the end of fourth grade seemed silly, now. "Hi, Claire," I said.

"I've got to find Ms. Morgan," she said, "so I can get started."

I listened to Claire breathing into the phone and still thinking about her summer project. Nothing had changed in Claire's life.

"I looked her up in the phone book," she continued, "but Katie, you won't believe how many Morgans there are in the phone book. What am I going to do?"

I picked loose paper clips off Dad's desk and tossed them at his magnetic paper-clip holder. I couldn't think of what to say.

"How can I get her thinking about marrying us," Claire continued, "if I can't find her?"

A little card on Dad's desk caught my eye. A red-haired lady in a stupid hat with a feather looked up at me. "Sadie Fowler, Real Estate," the card said. Ugh! I tossed the card at the magnet. Of course it stuck. It was a magnetic card.

"The only thing I can think of," Claire said, "is going to the library. She might actually be there. I want to go there tomorrow."

Dad came into his office and was pointing at his watch. "I'm expecting a call," he said.

"My father says I have to go to the library with someone." Claire drew a long breath. "Will you go with me, Katie?"

"I don't know if I can," I said. I pressed the phone against my cheek. "Are we still able to do normal things?" I asked Dad.

"Like what?" he asked.

I told him about Claire and the library. I didn't tell him about Claire's horrible plans for Ms. Morgan. "Of course you can do things like that," he said. In a few moments, we had it worked out. Mr. Plummer would take us at ten. Dad would get us at noon.

As soon as I put down the phone, it rang again. Dad picked it up. "Hello, Sadie," he said.

He started writing on a piece of paper.

"I'll see you at 10:30 tomorrow," I heard him say. I joined Tyler on the couch. We wrapped one of Grandma's knitted blankets around us.

"I don't want to move to Portland," I said.

"Me, neither," Tyler said. He leaned against me and stuck his thumb in his mouth.

Dad came back and sat beside us. "This won't be so bad," he said. "We can help each other make it work."

"What about Sierra?" I asked. "If we move, I'll never see her again."

"We'll make sure you get together for visits," Dad said.

Tyler looked up into Dad's face. "If Mommy was here, we wouldn't have to move. Mommy wouldn't let us move."

Dad set down his mug and pulled Tyler into his lap. "Your mommy could give us lessons on moving. She's traveling all the time."

"She should stop that," Tyler said. "Let's ask her to come home."

"Your mom and I don't live together anymore."

Dad rubbed his chin on Tyler's head. "If you lived with your mom, you wouldn't be with me. I would miss you too much."

I sighed. "Everything is awful," I said.

"I think we need something to take our mind off our troubles," Dad said. "Let's watch a movie."

Chapter 7

What Happened at the Library

Tyler is coming with us?" Claire backed up against her dad's car as if blocking it from us. She was wearing her sunglasses and a blue beret. Over her navy tights, she had on a long, pale-blue shirt with a wide belt.

"If he's with us, the house will stay cleaner." I didn't tell her the house needed to be clean so that Sadie, the real estate agent, would like it.

Claire frowned at Tyler. "Keep your shoes off the back seat," she said.

"Actually," I said, "he has to ride in his car seat. My dad is bringing it over."

Tyler stuck out his lower lip. "I'm going to read big books at the library."

"I am going to read poems," Claire said with a toss of her blond curls. She smoothed her blue shirt. "These are poet clothes I'm wearing."

"That looks like your dad's shirt," I said. "The sleeves are too long."

Claire rolled the sleeves up some more.

"Potes are silly." Tyler smoothed his own red shirt and tugged on his shorts.

Five-year-olds don't know what poets are, I thought, as we watched Dad fasten Tyler's car seat into the Plummer's car. Ms. Morgan had read poems to us at school. She would think it was great—Claire being a poet.

"Have a good time," Dad said. He ran back across the street. He had half an hour to finish tidying the house. Would the real estate person wear her stupid hat when she came to our house? Would our front yard have a For Sale sign on it when we got back?

Claire got into the front seat of her car and held up the litter bag. "If you have anything to throw away, it goes in here," she said. She held the bag in front of Tyler for a long time.

Tyler stared out the window and wouldn't look at her.

"We keep our car spotless," Claire said.

That was true. Claire's car looked brand-new. Ours had a brown stain in the front where Dad had spilled coffee, and a green stain in the back where Tyler threw up once after eating spinach.

"Good morning," Mr. Plummer said. "I've been pruning the roses. Big job." He slid into the front seat and checked his watch. "The library opens in three minutes."

"I'm going to read all kinds of poetry," Claire said. "And then, I'll write some."

"A good thing to do," Mr. Plummer said, glancing into the rearview mirror as he backed out of the driveway. "Reading good poetry trains your ear."

I pictured Claire's ear holding a pencil and giggled.

Claire frowned at me. I giggled again.

When we walked into the library, tons of people were already there. "I have to find out where they keep the poetry," Claire said. She went toward the librarian's desk, her head turning back and forth like a robot's head. I figured she was looking for Ms. Morgan—the real reason we were there.

Tyler tugged me into the children's section and rushed toward the shelves of picture books. "See you later," he called.

"Stay in the children's area," I told him.

"I don't want children's poetry," Claire was saying to the man at the reference desk. "I want grown-up poetry." He told her to go up the stairs and to the left.

"I'm looking for art books," I said to him. "Grown-up ones."

"Art books?" Claire turned back to me.

"Ms. Morgan likes artists, too," I said.

"You didn't wear the right clothes," she said, looking at my shorts and T-shirt.

"Artists can wear anything they want," I told her.

The man wrote down directions to the art section. "There are some good books in the children's room, as well," he said, "if these don't work for you."

As we climbed the stairs, I planned my next bird picture. I could give it to Ms. Morgan when school started up next fall. I stubbed my toe on the next step as I remembered we might not be here next fall. We might be living in Portland. Ms. Morgan might be living at Claire's!

Claire stopped to peer over the railing to the ground floor. "You can see more people from up here."

"Forget it, Claire," I said. "She's not here. It's a crazy idea."

Claire sighed. "It was all I could think of. We'll just have to come back every day until we find her." We moved to one side so a mother carrying a baby and a huge pile of books could get past us.

"I'm serious about the art books," I said, "even if you don't really care about poetry."

"I am very serious," Claire said. "Ms. Morgan will love having a poet for a daughter."

At the top of the stairs we split up. A few minutes later, I found art books. I was surprised! A lot of them were about drawing naked people. A lady with sharp glasses came to look at the art books, too, so I couldn't even peek into the naked ones.

Finally, I found a book on how to draw birds. Step-by-step instructions. I went downstairs and checked the big clock in the lobby. The real estate lady was at our house right now. All at once I wanted to be at home. Dad needed me there to remind him that the Portland idea was a bad one.

In the children's section, Tyler was sitting in a nest of picture books. His fingers were on the pictures, and he was telling stories about them to a baby snoozing in a stroller beside him. "You can't take that many books home," I told him.

"Be quiet," he said. "This baby is sleeping. His mother is right over there." He pointed to a woman who waved and smiled at me.

I moved down the rows of little-kid books to the novels. I pulled them out and read the first pages and the last pages to see if they were any good. I wondered if there were any books about kids having to move. Probably not. It was too terrible to read about.

When I checked on him again, Tyler was sitting in the window seat next to a big kid.

The flannel shirt looked familiar. Alex Ramirez!

Alex looked up. "Hi Katie," he said. "Is this your brother? He sure likes bridges." He tapped the book that was spread across their laps. "Famous Suspension Bridges of the World."

"Go away, Katie," Tyler said. "We're busy."

"Dad told me to check on you a lot," I told him.

"I'll watch him for a while," Alex said. "He's pretty fun."

"Next bridge," Tyler said. They both looked down as Alex turned the page.

As I went upstairs to find Claire, I once again saw the big clock. "You must not move to Portland," the real estate person might be saying to Dad. She would pull on her feathered hat and wave a big purse at him. "Okay," Dad would say. And that would be that.

In the shelves marked "NORTHWEST TRAVEL," someone with a long, brown ponytail was pulling books off the shelf. Unbelievable! Ms. Morgan was here!

I scooted out of sight around the corner.

The minute she saw her, Claire would start her project—working on Ms. Morgan to be her mother. I had to get Claire out of the library!

I ducked around the crafts section and into biographies. At last I found her, turning the pages of a fat book.

"We have to go now," I told her. "It's almost noon."

She looked at her silver-and-blue watch. "We have ten more minutes."

"Dad hates waiting," I told her. "He gets furious."

With a sigh, Claire straightened her blue shirt. She put on her dark glasses and her beret. At last, she turned toward the stairs, but she stopped to peer down every row of books. "I've been looking every five minutes," she said. "I'm so sad she didn't come."

"Come on," I said as I walked fast to the stairs.

Tyler was playing a hide-and-seek game on the computer. It took forever for him to finish. Then Claire and I had to find the books he wanted to take home. "You're so crabby," he told me as we finally stood in the check-out line.

After checking out, I herded Claire and Tyler toward the front doors. We were almost out! Ms. Morgan would be safe for one more day.

"Oh my gosh." Claire screeched to a halt. "There she is!" She raced back across the lobby.

Ms. Morgan was coming down the stairs. She looked up when she heard Claire's voice. "What a surprise," she said, smiling at all of us.

"Hi, Ms. Morgan," I called. "We have to go. Dad's probably out in front right now." I pushed Tyler through the door.

"Quit that," Tyler said, and all his picture books crashed onto my feet. "Quit pushing me," he yelled.

In the checkout line, people turned to watch Tyler and me. But Claire stood close to Ms. Morgan, showing her the poetry books. Ms. Morgan smiled and nodded at her.

Her smile looked very motherly.

Chapter 8

A Surprising Invitation

"How come we have to wait for Dad out here?" Tyler asked. He dumped his books onto a bench next to the big planter and squinted at the cars going by on Monroe Street. "He's not even here."

"We just have to," I said. I peeked inside to see Claire and Ms. Morgan still side-by-side in the line. I stacked my books next to Tyler's and thumped myself down on the bench. I crossed my arms and stared at the library wall. Only Dad could save Ms. Morgan from Claire, I thought, and Dad was always late.

A few minutes later, Claire and Ms. Morgan joined us on the sunny library terrace. They didn't look like a mother and daughter yet. They looked ordinary.

"What are you reading?" Ms. Morgan asked Tyler.

"Books about mothers," he answered. He lifted the books up so Ms. Morgan could see the covers. Sure enough, every one of the books was about some kind of mother. Mother owls, mother monkeys, mother chickens, mother cows.

"Hmm," Ms. Morgan said, looking into Tyler's face with a kind smile.

He grinned at her. "I can read them myself."

"Ahem," I said.

"I can read big parts of them." He glared at me, and his red hair bristled in the sunshine.

"Hello, everyone." It was Dad, striding up the steps, all dressed up. "Ms. Morgan," he said with a big smile. "We didn't expect to run into you today."

"Nice to see you," she said. She held out her hand to shake Dad's. "We don't need to be so formal now that Katie's in fifth grade. Please call me Janna."

"Happy to do that," Dad said. "If you'll call me Bill."

Janna! A delicious name! I bumped Claire's arm, but she didn't notice. She was staring at Ms. Morgan with a sappy smile on her face.

"I'm going to get to know Oregon this summer," Ms. Morgan said. She held out her books. "This is a great one. Oregon Hiking Trails. I can't wait to go hiking and backpacking."

"Oregon has great trails," Dad said.

"I like hiking," Claire said, standing between Ms. Morgan and Dad and looking up into Ms. Morgan's face.

"And this book," Ms. Morgan said as she held out another, "is about all the parks. I just found out that Silver Falls State Park is not far away. I want to see those waterfalls."

"The last time I went there, Katie was a baby," Dad said.

"We should go there," Claire said.

Dad nodded his head at Claire. "We should

plan a picnic," he said to Ms. Morgan. "Would you like to go with us to Silver Falls?"

Ms. Morgan nodded. "I'd love to." She wasn't acting at all like a teacher today.

"Great idea," Claire said. She nodded at my dad as if he were her dad.

"When should we go?" Ms. Morgan asked. She pushed her ponytail over her shoulder and smiled at Tyler and me.

"Our life is a bit up in the air right now," Dad said, and I wondered again about what the real estate lady might have said. Was the For Sale sign in our front yard?

Then I forgot about our house as I looked at Ms. Morgan smiling at Dad. Maybe Claire's project wouldn't work. Maybe Ms. Morgan would chose my dad, not Claire's. I moved close to Dad and leaned against him.

"This weekend?" Dad asked.

Claire placed her hand on my dad's arm. "That sounds perfect," she said.

Dad looked down at her and said, "Claire, you and your dad should come, too."

"Too many people," I said, putting my hand on his other arm.

"We would love to," Claire murmured.

"There's not room in the car." I tugged on Dad's shirt sleeve.

Dad gave me the look. He didn't know about Claire's project. "I'm sure we can work out some driving arrangements, Katie. Shall we go tomorrow? Saturday?"

"I'll bring potato salad," Ms. Morgan said. After a few more plans were made, she waved good-bye and walked to the bike racks.

"She rode a bike here," Claire said, clasping her hands together.

"People ride bikes around here," I said. I gathered up my books and some of Tyler's.

"I never thought she would." Claire gazed at Ms. Morgan as if she were someone really famous. Finally, she picked up her books and started down the steps to the sidewalk.

"She's not old," I said. "Even Dad rides a bike."

"Wish I had more time to ride," Dad said

as he opened the car doors. As we climbed in, I hoped Claire wouldn't notice the banana peel that was stuck between the front seats. I didn't need to worry. She was too busy cranking her head around to watch Ms. Morgan.

"Alex Ramirez!" Claire fell backwards against the car seat and pointed out the window.

Alex was running down the library steps, his flannel shirt flapping around his legs. He went straight to the bike rack where Ms. Morgan waited.

He showed her his books, and they started laughing about something. Then, they both got on their bikes and peddled away.

Chapter 9

Claire's Project: The Next Step

"I can't believe it," Claire kept saying. "Alex was with Ms. Morgan."

"That's my friend," Tyler said. "He's just like me. He likes bridges."

"Maybe they live near each other," I told Claire.

As Dad turned the car into our street I looked to see if there was a sign in front of our house. There wasn't.

"Well, anyway," Claire said, "I'm going to make a list for our picnic." She got out of the car and started toward her house.

"We should make a list, too," Dad said, "of all the things we have to do if I take a different job." He unfastened Tyler from his car seat.

"Is it definite?" I asked. "Are we going to move?"

"It's not definite. I'm only getting information. Just in case." He set Tyler down in the driveway and piled books into his arms. "But we have work to do. The realtor said no one can see the 'lines' of our house."

"What does that mean?" I asked. "Lines?"

"If there's too much clutter, you can't see how big a house is. Or if it's nice."

"This porch doesn't have any lines at all," I said, stepping over Tyler's pedal car. "Tyler has way too many toys."

"No way!" Tyler roared. He pushed out his lower lip.

"We all have to get rid of things," Dad said.

I nodded my head at him. "Especially your stuff, Dad. All those fishing poles you never use."

He held the door open for us. "I want the three of us to work together on this," he said sternly. "I want us to act like a family."

While he fixed peanut butter sandwiches, Dad talked about easy things we could get rid of—things nobody cared about. "Those old paper bags in the cupboard," he said. "They can go to recycling. And the cardboard boxes in the utility room. I'll flatten them."

"After the utility room," I said, "we'll be done."

"Katie," Dad started, but then the phone rang.

It was Claire.

"My father says I shouldn't expect him to fall in love with Ms. Morgan," she said. "But I can tell he likes her, so I haven't given up."

I kicked a piece of carrot under the refrigerator with the toe of my sandal. Lucky thing Dad hadn't seen me do that. I bent over to see where the carrot had gone.

"He says she was a special teacher, so our picnic should be special. Not ordinary."

"Huh?" The carrot was out of sight. It was going to rot under there. I stood back up.

"We are going to make fancy sandwiches," Claire continued. "What are you bringing?"

I tucked the phone under my chin. “What are we taking to the picnic?” I asked Dad.

“A watermelon?” he asked.

Claire sighed when I told her. “Watermelon is ordinary, Katie.”

“We like watermelon,” I said.

“Tell your dad we’ll bring the cutlery,” she said. “We want things to match.”

“What’s cuttle ree?”

“Cut-ler-ee. Forks and knives and spoons,” she said. “Really, Katie. When you don’t have a mother at home, you have to learn about things like cutlery.”

I hung up. Almost immediately, the phone rang again.

“I wasn’t done,” Claire said. “I’m sure Ms. Morgan would like to ride in our car. I noticed your dad’s car was a little messy.”

I slammed the phone down.

Chapter 10

Too Much to Think About

The telephone was still bouncing on the counter when Dad walked by. “Whoa,” he said. “That’s not the way to handle the phone.”

“Claire says our car is messy.” I stomped behind him into the kitchen. “And she doesn’t think watermelon is fancy enough.”

Dad raised his hands. “She’s right about the car. But watermelon sounds great to me.”

“Watermelon is very great,” Tyler said as he carried all his library books into the kitchen. He set his books down in the middle of the floor and opened one. “Read to me, Katie.”

"Not now," I said. I rubbed my forehead. It was sore from too many worries.

Dad put the peanut butter sandwiches onto paper napkins and took them to the table.

"I want Ms. Morgan to ride with us," I said. "It's our picnic. Not Claire's."

He poured milk for us and water for him. "I'll vacuum the car."

"You should spruce it," Tyler said.

"Okay," Dad said. "I'll spruce it. Wash your hands, Katie and Tyler."

"There's too much to think about," I said as we sat down at the table. "We're supposed to be kids on summer vacation. Having fun." I sniffed at the peanut butter in my sandwich.

Dad leaned back in his chair. "The picnic will be a nice break from fixing up our house. According to Sadie, we really need to clear things out. If we end up not moving, at least our house will feel bigger."

"I hope that company doesn't want you." I ripped my sandwich into little pieces and counted them. Ten little peanut butter sandwiches.

"That's not supportive," Dad said. He chewed and swallowed. "I'd like to have you kids rooting for me instead of making it harder." Tyler was squeezing his sandwich and licking the peanut butter that oozed out.

I thought about rooting for Dad. I touched his arm. "Mr. Flagstaff likes you. He'll be sad if you get a different job."

"I need to have a talk with him before I make any decisions. He gets back Tuesday." He smiled at me. "But that's my girl. That's the kind of help I need."

I popped one of my little sandwiches into my mouth and chewed. "The picnic was your idea," I said. "Why is Claire in charge of it now?"

Tyler zoomed a piece of his sandwich across his plate, making sounds like squealing tires. "The winner!" he announced, and popped the piece of sandwich into his mouth.

Dad reached across the table to touch my hand. "The picnic will be fine," he said. "We can eat, take some walks to see the falls, and then come home." He grinned at me. "A picnic is a picnic."

After Tyler was down for his nap, Dad started stacking newspapers in the utility room. I wandered down the hall and into my room. My orange polka-dot bedspreads glowed on the twin beds. My shell collection looked pretty on top of my bookcase. Real Estate Sadie would say my room had plenty of lines. It was perfect.

Maybe my closet had some extra stuff. I looked in. Pants and shirts lay in heaps on the floor; papers and puzzles and games spilled across the shelves. Sadie would not like my closet, but I did. Everything was right where I could find it.

Next to the closet door, my poster of Mom holding her guitar filled the whole wall. She and Dad had been divorced for more than three years. We spent time with her at Christmas and in the summer, but I missed her, especially at night after Dad tucked me in. "I'll turn the light off myself," I always said. "I have to look at Mom first."

He would nod and get a sad look on his face before he went out and closed my door.

I knew she was only a poster, but I told her everything. I pretended she could whisper back to me.

I traced her smile with my finger. "Do we have to move to Portland?" I asked her.

She didn't answer. She hardly ever spoke to me in the daytime.

I flopped onto my bed and stared at her. "What about Claire's summer project?" I asked. Mom still didn't say anything, but her smile reminded me that she was still there for me. I still had a mom. We could talk on the phone. I could listen to her CDs. When we got together, she would read to us and hug us. Claire's mom couldn't do any of that. She could never step out of the old photo Claire had showed me once.

I sat up on the bed; my mind was made up. Claire needed a new mom much more than I did. Ms. Morgan should live across the street. Claire was going to be the perfect daughter for her.

Chapter 11

Mom on the Phone

That night after supper, Dad went to the store to buy the watermelon. "Back in ten minutes," he said.

I got out the family photo album. Tyler curled up beside me in the green chair. "This is Mom when you were still inside her," I told him.

He touched Mom's big belly with his finger. "I want her back with us," Tyler said. He pushed the album away and stuck his thumb in his mouth.

"Dad says she's too famous now," I told him. "She can't come back."

"She could sing 'Down in the Valley' when I go to bed," he said around his thumb. "She sings that when we're at Grandma's house."

"She sings it to me, too," I said. Mom was also good at rubbing my back to help me fall asleep.

Tyler pulled the album back and turned the page to a photo of Mom sitting in a circle of people playing guitars. "Who are those people?" Tyler poked at the photos with his wet thumb.

"They came every Thursday night." I wiped thumb juice off the photo. "They played music in the family room."

"If Mom was here, I would be in my bed listening to that." He turned another page. "There!" he said. "She got me out of her stomach."

Mom was holding Tyler, a tiny baby, in her arms. Her face looked soft as she bent over him. She looked really happy, being a mother.

I remembered her in the kitchen, sprinkling cinnamon on my French toast. I remembered her picking me up at school, leaning out of the car and saying, "Hurry up, Katie bug."

Beside me, Tyler sucked harder on his thumb. I was going to have to tell Dad about the thumb. He would say Tyler was going through a stage. He would tell me Tyler needs lots of hugs right now.

As I closed the album, the phone rang.

"You have to get it," Tyler said. "Dad's not here."

I ran to the phone. "Hi, Katie bug," Mom's voice said.

"Mom!"

Tyler ran into the family room. "Let me," he shouted. "Let me talk!"

I jerked the phone away from him. Then I gave up. No way could I talk to Mom while he was yelling. I slid down on the floor and thumped my feet while he pressed the phone against his ear and nodded.

"Say something to her," I whispered. He shook his head and frowned at me.

When Mom's voice stopped, I held out my hand. "My turn," I said.

Tyler shook his head. "Mommy?" he asked. "Can you come back home?"

Mom's voice started up again and I heard something about concerts and Dad. "She wants to talk to Dad," I said. "Give me the phone."

"She's coming," Tyler said as he handed the phone to me. "I think."

"Hi, Mom," I said.

"Katie." As usual Mom's talking sounded almost like her singing. "I'm doing a concert in Oregon. Next week. It would be so much fun to see you all."

My stomach lurched with excitement. "I'll tell Dad!"

"Where is he?" she asked. "I want to talk to you, too, but can you call him to the phone?"

The back door opened, and Dad came in carrying a huge watermelon. "He's here," I said.

He rolled the watermelon onto the kitchen counter and raised his eyebrows at me.

"It's Mommy!" Tyler yelled. "I think she's coming home!"

Dad picked up the phone. "Hello, Roxie."

Tyler and I sat on the floor while Dad talked to Mom. "Great!" he kept saying. "Great! Okay to bring a five-year-old?"

Finally he handed the phone to me. "She says it's your turn."

"Honey," Mom said. "I'll see you next week at my concert."

My poster picture of Mom holding her guitar flew into my mind. "Cool," I said.

"And then we'll have supper together," Mom said. "What should I order?"

"Pizza," I told her. Beside me, Tyler jiggled up and down. "Don't get mushrooms," I said. "Remember? I hate mushrooms."

Mom laughed. "I can't wait to see you."

She told me about a boat ride she took on the Mississippi River. "I thought about Huck Finn and Tom Sawyer," she said. "Ask your dad who they are." She went on about a concert she did in North Carolina the week before. "My agent thinks my next CD will get me an award," Mom said. "It's pretty exciting here." As we hung up, I thought of all the things I should have told her. About my new art book. About tomorrow's picnic. "Does she know we might have to move?" I asked Dad.

He shook his head. "We'll have lots to talk about when we see her." He picked up the watermelon. "How am I going to fit this into the refrigerator?"

While Dad was moving things around in the refrigerator, Tyler and I did jumping jacks across the kitchen. "She's coming. She's coming," Tyler sang.

Dad pulled more things out of a grocery bag. "Napkins and paper plates," he said. "For the picnic."

"Those plates aren't fancy enough," I told him.

He looked surprised, but I didn't feel like telling him I had decided that Claire's plans for Ms. Morgan were okay.

"We can decorate these," I told Tyler. A moment later, he and I were drawing on the plates with my colored pencils. I drew a beautiful bluebird for Ms. Morgan while Tyler filled a bunch of plates with crawly black ants.

Chapter 12

The Picnic

We were in the driveway, loading things into the car, when Ms. Morgan pedaled up the street. She grinned as she whooshed into our driveway.

Ms. Morgan at my house! She hugged me, and then Tyler. "Great day for a picnic," she said.

Today she was wearing shorts. She pulled off her bike helmet and put on a red ball cap that matched her shirt. She saw me looking at her hiking boots and stuck out her foot. "These are brand new," she said. "I'm trying to break them in so they'll feel comfortable when I go on a long hike."

She undid the bungee cords that held a large bowl onto the rack of her bike. “I’m so glad this didn’t spill off,” she said as she handed it to me. “I’m afraid I took a chance with our potato salad.”

Dad took the bowl and put it into our cooler. “It’s safe now,” he said. “Nice bicycle. I’ll have to show you mine sometime.”

“Dad has so many bicycles, we can’t put the car in the garage anymore,” I said.

“She’s right,” Dad said. “Isn’t that embarrassing?”

“Good morning.” Mr. Plummer marched up our driveway, looking as if he’d just stepped out of a store, in white shorts and a bright, flowered shirt. Claire followed in blue tennis shoes, blue shorts, a blue crop top, and even a blue barrette in her blond hair. She smiled sweetly at Ms. Morgan.

“I put the sandwich fixings into our cooler,” Mr. Plummer said. “And there’s probably room in there for the salad.”

“We found a place for the salad.” Ms. Morgan waved her hand at Dad’s cooler. “We picked perfect weather, didn’t we?”

Dad fitted bags full of paper plates, potato chips, and mystery stuff I hoped were cookies into the trunk. “Let’s hit the road,” he said.

“Ahem,” Mr. Plummer said. “Unfortunately, we will need two cars.”

“We certainly can’t all go in yours,” Claire said. She glanced into our car as if she expected something nasty to fly out of it.

“Ms. Morgan should ride with Claire and me,” Mr. Plummer said. “We’ll meet up at the park.”

“Good idea,” Dad said.

“Yay!” Claire grabbed Ms. Morgan’s hand.

Ms. Morgan hesitated. “Will that be all right?” she asked.

“Of course.” Dad lifted Tyler into his car seat. “We’ll be more comfortable. But then, to be fair, I hope you’ll ride with us on the way back.”

Ms. Morgan smiled at him. “Of course.” She went across the street with the Plummers.

We drove for ages while I watched the Plummer’s car ahead of us, wishing I could hear what they were talking about, wishing I had gone with them, wishing Ms. Morgan didn’t have to be Claire's mother. Finally our cars drove up a narrow road through tall evergreens. When I opened the car door, I heard sounds of a crashing waterfall.

"Fifteen different falls," Mr. Plummer was saying when we all stood together in the parking lot. "We can hike to several of them."

"Let's hike right now," I said. "Ms. Morgan has on her new hiking boots."

Dad pulled binoculars out of their case and hung the strap around his neck. "Shall we work up an appetite?"

Mr. Plummer reached into his car. "I brought a camera," he said.

Claire stood very still. "I think we could stay here on the nice grass," she said. "I brought my latest poetry."

"After we hike," Ms. Morgan said, "we'll have more things to write about."

Claire sighed, but she came with us when we crossed the grassy picnic area to stand by the rushing river. We threw sticks into the water and watched them float downstream where they disappeared over a cliff. Ms. Morgan took Tyler's hand firmly in hers. "This is no time for a swim," she told Tyler.

"There's a fence to keep people from going over the falls," I said.

"But still," Ms. Morgan said, "we don't want to lose Tyler for one minute." She grinned at him, and he smiled back.

"You've made a friend," Dad said.

"Aren't we too close to this wild river?" Claire asked.

"That's the whole idea," I told her. "That's why we came."

Tyler led us down the trail, and Claire ran beside him, trying to stay as close as possible to Ms. Morgan.

Chapter 13

Disaster on the Trail

The trail led us steeply down until we reached the foot of the first waterfall. Mist floated around us as we tipped our heads back to see the top of the falls.

"My neck hurts." Dad wiggled his head to get the kinks out and picked up the binoculars. "Look there," he said, pointing across the river. "A water ouzel. That bird is hunting for food. It knows how to swim under water. It even knows how to walk on the bottom of the river."

All at once Tyler's thumb was in his mouth. "That bird," he said removing his thumb a quick moment, "is looking for his mother."

"How do you know that?" Ms. Morgan asked.

"All the children are looking and looking," he told her. "Expec-shally." He always had trouble with that word. "Expec-shally if their mothers are gone away. That story is in all my books."

Ms. Morgan looked over at Dad, who looked worried. "You may be right," she said to Tyler. "My mother lives a long way from here in Minnesota. I send her lots of e-mails."

Tyler popped his thumb out of his mouth and wiped it on his shirt. "More waterfalls," he yelled, pointing downriver. We hiked down the trail and reached a place where we could actually walk behind some falls. The river roared over and past us like a giant's shower.

Claire pulled her light jacket around her. "Drippy under here."

"Smile," Mr. Plummer said, lifting his camera.

"Take another one," Claire said. She pulled Ms. Morgan over to a boulder and posed beside her, tipping her head like a movie star. Mr. Plummer snapped the picture. They looked like a perfect mother and daughter.

After the fourth waterfall, Dad said he was starving, and Ms. Morgan said her new boots were starting to hurt.

As we climbed back up the cliffs toward the picnic grounds, Ms. Morgan stopped at a bend in the trail and fanned herself. "Look at these lovely mosses," she said. As she trailed her fingers through the green plants growing between the rocks, Mr. Plummer rushed over with his camera.

Above us, some birds began to sing.

"I wish I could see those birds." Dad balanced himself against a tree trunk and held the binoculars up to his eyes.

"Let me look, Daddy," Tyler said. Dad held the binoculars in front of Tyler, but no matter what he did, Tyler said everything was black.

I kept walking up the zigzag path, careful to stay away from the side that sloped down toward the noisy river. On the uphill side, ferns and rocks looked like a perfect place to find a mouse or a ground squirrel. I studied little holes and dark places under the ferns until, all at once, I realized a huge slug was draped across some sticks. It was looking back at me. I swallowed a scream. Then I looked closer at his orange-and-black stripes.

"You're beautiful," I told the slug. "And big. Almost as big as my shoe."

I found a leaf and slid it under the slug's head. "Climb on," I told him, but he pulled back and wouldn't move.

"Come on, guy." I gently poked his tail with a stick, and sure enough, he moved a little. "Come see this," I called to the others.

Mr. Plummer was trying to get Tyler to look at the birds through the camera instead of the binoculars. "Just look," Mr. Plummer kept saying. "No fingerprints, please."

"Let's try the binoculars again," Dad said. "I don't care if he gets fingerprints on those."

"Never mind." Tyler pushed the binoculars away.

By then, I had two sticks. The more I gently poked his tail, the more the slug crawled toward me, getting on top of the second stick, leaving silver slime behind as he went. "This is better than a bird," I yelled back to the others. "Hurry!"

As they started toward me, I pulled on the stick, and the slug held on. But then, my stick bent under the weight of it. I heaved up, and all at once, the end of that stick popped and, just like a golf club, sent the slug flying into the air. It flew straight toward Ms. Morgan!

Ms. Morgan's boots slid and stumbled on the path. Her eyes widened, and she raised her hands. Was she going to catch that slug? Slime and all?

No, she wasn't. With a soft plop, the slug hit her in the stomach and thunked to the ground. "Oh," she said as her feet finally slipped out from under her on the downhill side of the path.

Her bottom thunked down onto the ferns, and she slid away. In a moment, she had disappeared.

Still holding the stick, I stared at where Ms. Morgan had been. My mouth was open, but my voice was stuck.

I turned away from all the scandalized faces and ran up the trail toward the parking lot.

Our picnic was ruined!

Chapter 14

Claire's Project: Moving Right Along

By the time I reached the sunshine of the picnic area, loud, gasping noises were coming out of my mouth. I flopped down on the grass and buried my face in my arms. Over and over in my mind, the orange-and-black slug flew toward Ms. Morgan. Over and over, I watched her slide down the steep bank beside the trail.

What if she'd broken something? A leg. An arm. They were probably calling on their cell phones, getting an ambulance. She would go to the hospital. I loved her so much, and now, I knew for sure that I wanted her to be my mother.

My mother. Not Claire's.

I had ruined everything. Now, she would be sure to choose Claire. Every time she thought about me, she would remember that slug.

I could hear them coming back. I peeked through the blades of grass and saw that Dad was carrying Tyler, who was carrying the binoculars. He looked through them at Dad's head. "There's something black in your ear," he yelled.

"Quit that," Dad said. But he was laughing.

He sounded normal. Maybe everything wasn't ruined, after all.

Ms. Morgan walked next to Claire. They were holding hands while Claire told her a story about a trip she had taken. Claire would never have picked up a slug. She would have walked right past it. Claire never did terrible things.

Ms. Morgan was walking fine. Her arms looked okay. She was even smiling. At Claire. I buried my face again in the grass as despair washed over me.

“Let’s get the picnic things,” I heard Mr. Plummer say, and he organized everyone into carrying things from the car.

Dad bent over me. “Once you’ve apologized, you’ll feel better,” he said. He went off toward our car.

I sat up on the grass. Finally, I got to my feet.

“Wait,” Mr. Plummer was saying. “The cloth goes on first.” He pulled a green-and-blue cloth from a box and tossed it over the wooden table. He lifted the lid of one of the coolers. With a flourish, he pulled out a bud vase holding a white rose.

Thoughts of last Thanksgiving flew into my mind. I remembered how Claire and her dad had decorated their whole house. Was our picnic going to be decorated the same way?

While everyone was looking at the rose, I moved close to Ms. Morgan. “I’m really sorry,” I said. “I didn’t mean for that slug to fly at you.”

She smiled down at me. “That was a slug out of control,” she said. “It was actually quite pretty, once we took a good look at it.”

I blinked the tears from my eyes. "You thought it was pretty?"

She nodded. "Claire's dad took pictures."

I touched her arm. "Did you hurt yourself when you fell?"

She brushed at the back of her shorts. "Only my dignity," she said with a grin. "I'm fine."

"Great!" I said.

I ran to our car to get a paper bag Dad was holding. "Tyler and I made the plates fancy," I said when I got back. "I made a bluebird for you, Ms. Morgan."

She held it up to admire it. "This is much too beautiful to put food on. I want to save it."

"I can make another one for you," I told her. "It's easy."

"We brought some real plates," Claire said as her dad carried another box to the table. "Real plates don't bend."

Claire and I set the real plates on the table.

"First, we have hors d'oeuvres," Mr. Plummer said. "Ta-da!" He opened a cooler and pulled out a platter of fancy vegetables and gooey sauces to dip them in.

"We brought some chips," I said, pulling a crackly bag out of our box.

As Claire looked at the potato chips, I could tell she was thinking that they were ordinary. She opened the other cooler. "My father and I made these this morning." The tray she held was full of tiny stuffed tomatoes.

I set down the bag of chips.

Ms. Morgan picked up a stuffed tomato. "Clever," she said before she popped it into her mouth.

"Did you bring peanut butter sandwiches?" Tyler asked.

"Assorted meats. Three kinds of cheese." Claire slid onto the bench close to Ms. Morgan and smiled up at her. "I love helping in the kitchen."

"These are certainly good," Ms. Morgan said as she reached for another little tomato.

Dad handed me a package. "Here, Katie. Want to give everyone a paper cup?"

"Just a minute," Mr. Plummer said. He opened a cardboard box and lifted out wine goblets—glass ones with stems. "I had some extra room in the car, so I put them in." He stopped then and looked at Tyler.

"Can I have a pretty glass, too?" Tyler's blue eyes were full of wishes.

"Use two hands," Dad said. He twisted open the thermos and poured lemonade into the tall glasses.

"Good thing we remembered the ice," Mr. Plummer said. He lifted ice cubes from a thermos bowl with silver tongs and plunked them lightly into the drinks.

Ms. Morgan lifted her glass and the ice cubes clinked against the sides. "Let's toast to this wonderful day in a beautiful place."

"First, a picture," Mr. Plummer said. As we held our glasses up for the toast, he rummaged through all his pockets for the camera. Claire slid across the bench, closer to Ms. Morgan.

He snapped three pictures, and then handed the camera to Dad. "I wonder if you would take one with me in it," he said.

Mr. Plummer crowded onto the bench so he and Claire and Ms. Morgan were in a row.

"Smile," Dad said. He snapped a quick photo. At last, we could quit holding our glasses up in the air.

Even Tyler joined in the toast, the beautiful glass shaking in his little hands.

Chapter 15

Tyler's Wish

Tyler opened up his sandwich and put the parts all over his plate. "My mother is coming to live with us," he said. "She's going to be our mother again."

"Um," Dad said. He had just taken a big bite of his chicken sandwich.

"No, she isn't," I said.

Dad finally swallowed. "She's coming to Portland next week to do a concert. We're going to it." It was short notice, he said, because Mom was filling in for another singer who was sick.

"Katie's mom is on a poster in her bedroom," Claire said. "She's wearing a beautiful red vest that sparkles. I wish she would come back to live with you."

"She will," Tyler said. "She's going to cook my breakfast."

Dad frowned. "We're going to her concert, Tyler. Then we'll come home, and she'll go do her next concert."

"I guess she has CDs out?" Mr. Plummer asked.

"Four CDs," I said around my bite of sandwich. I stared across the table at the three of them, Ms. Morgan, Mr. Plummer, and Claire, looking like a family as they sat side-by-side at the picnic table. Ms. Morgan would probably like having a daughter who never talked with her mouth full.

"I wonder if there are any tickets left," Ms. Morgan said.

"I want to go to her concert," Claire said.

Tyler ripped his piece of ham into little pieces and made a tower on his plate.

"Eat your castle," Dad said.

"Lighthouse," Tyler said. "Blink, blink." He looked around at us. "The light goes on and off," he explained. "It blinks."

"I'll see if I can get more tickets," Dad said. "Unfortunately, we wouldn't be able to travel together," he continued, "because we're going to stay after the concert to visit with her."

"She's going to be my mother again," Tyler said, "and tuck me in."

Dad shook his head at Tyler. Then he swept his arm around him and held him close. "Your mom is really busy doing her concerts," he said.

Mr. Plummer and Dad shook their heads at each other and looked sad, feeling bad about Tyler, I guessed. They had forgotten that I missed Mom, too.

Ms. Morgan got up to make another sandwich. "This cheese is perfect with the ham," she said.

"Your potato salad is perfect with our sandwiches," Mr. Plummer said.

Claire ran around the table to watch Ms. Morgan build her sandwich. "My father is a wonderful cook."

Mr. Plummer coughed. “Well,” he said, “I do enjoy fussing around in the kitchen. But I could use new ideas for things to make.”

The grown-ups talked about recipes while we finished our sandwiches. Then, we played with Tyler’s Nerf ball and hit a badminton birdie around with the rackets the Plummers had brought. After that, we ate our watermelon and spit seeds into the grass, except for Claire, who folded her seeds into her paper napkin. Shadows of the tall trees filled the parking lot as we carried our boxes and bags to the cars.

After we said good-bye to Claire and Mr. Plummer, Tyler and I climbed into the back seat. Ms. Morgan sat in front with Dad. As we drove out of the park, I watched the back of Ms. Morgan’s head as she and Dad talked. Her head looked perfect in our front seat.

Dad was saying something about looking for another job and maybe having to move. He sounded worried again. Ms. Morgan said she liked living in Hartsdale, but it had taken a while to feel at home.

"Time to rise and shine." Dad's voice woke me up. I blinked at him. We were in our driveway. Beside me, Tyler stretched and yawned. "I want to go on the picnic," he said.

"You already went on the picnic." Dad unbuckled Tyler from his car seat.

"Where's Ms. Morgan?" I asked. Then, I saw her, unlocking her bike.

"I had a good time," she said as she pushed her bike toward us. "Thank you so much for inviting me." She swung her leg over the seat.

"I'll let you know about the tickets," Dad said to her. She waved at us and pedaled down the street.

I slammed the car door. "I fell asleep and missed her riding with us," I said as Dad handed me two grocery bags to carry into the house. "It was an awful picnic."

"I had a great time," Dad said.

"Claire is a pain," I said. I dropped the bags on the kitchen floor. "Did you see her trying to get Ms. Morgan to be her new mother?"

Dad stopped rinsing out a thermos and looked at me. "I can tell she really likes Ms. Morgan. How do you feel about that?"

Mixed-up thoughts chased around in my mind. Ms. Morgan and Claire looking perfect together. Mom, who was going to always be my mom, but was never coming back to stay with us. "I don't like it." I heaved a sigh. "I don't know."

He stared out the kitchen window as water continued to run into the sink. He spoke softly. "She has a very pretty smile." Finally, he turned the water off, but he didn't turn around.

I was pretty sure he was talking about Ms. Morgan.

A package of chocolate cookies stuck out of the grocery bag. I pulled them the rest of the way out. "How come we didn't eat these?"

"We were too stuffed." Dad took the cookies from me and tossed them into the high cupboard. "We'll save them for the next picnic," he said. "Don't tell you-know-who where they are."

Tyler had finally crawled out of the car and

stood yawning at the back door. "Don't tell me what?" he asked, blinking his blue eyes at us.

"Did you have enough to eat?" Dad asked.

Tyler rubbed his stomach, stuck it far out, and looked down at it. "It's full," he said.

"Thank goodness," Dad said. "We finally filled you up, Tyler."

Tyler walked around the kitchen, sticking his stomach out as far as he could. "Is tonight the concert?" he asked.

"Thursday," Dad said. He counted on his fingers. "Five more days." He went out the door to lock up the car.

"Five more days," Tyler said to me. "Mommy will come home then."

I sighed. "You didn't listen to Dad, Tyler. She's coming for the concert, and that's all."

Tears burst out of Tyler's eyes. "You're wrong, Katie. And you're bad." He stuck his thumb into his mouth and then popped it out. "You don't even want Mom anymore."

But I do! I thought. I dragged down the hall with him sniffling behind me. Was something wrong with me that made me keep thinking about hugging Ms. Morgan? I did want Mom back. I did.

I could almost feel Mom coming out of the bedroom, walking down the hall to us. Shaking her finger at us, telling us to stop arguing and get ready for bed. Happy tears rushed into my eyes as I pictured her here with us.

"Maybe she will come back," I told him. "Maybe she will."

Chapter 16

My Sad Life

On Monday, Dad was talking again about getting rid of extra stuff. "Janna Morgan says there's a good place to take clothes and toys we're not using," he told us. "It's a place where people who are poor can come and get free things." He set a desk lamp next to a stack of folded shirts on the family room floor. "The clothes need to be clean. Not worn out."

I went to my room and picked up the first thing I almost stepped on. My red-and-black T-shirt. Maybe someone else would like this shirt. But would she love it the way I loved it? It had a black Sharpie mark on the front, but I thought the mark looked like part of the design. I took it to the family room and put it next to Dad's pile.

Tyler came down the hall dragging a set of Lincoln Logs.

"You're giving those away?"

"No way," he answered. "I'm going to build a garage for my little trucks to live in."

I stopped at Dad's office and looked in. "Tyler's just playing," I told him.

He shook his head at me and pointed me back to my room.

After looking in my closet, I remembered the mother-mouse hotel behind the couch. Tyler said he was done playing with it. I found three pairs of shoes that didn't fit and a pair of boots that made a nasty, squeaky noise. I put them on the family room piles. Maybe Dad would be happy with me now.

By then, Dad had added a computer keyboard and some file boxes. "My office looks bigger now," he said with a grin. "It's beginning to have lines!"

"I hate lines," I said.

He looked at my pile. "Is that all you could find?"

I stomped down the hall and sat on my bed. Summer vacation wasn't supposed to be this horrible. Suddenly, I missed Sierra so much. If I moved away to Portland, would she remember me? Would we ever have another sleepover together? Would we ride our bikes to each other's houses the way we had planned?

I lay down on my bed and hugged my pillow. How could I live without Sierra? I loved the way she crinkled her freckled nose. The way she snorted when she laughed. I loved the way she jiggled up and down when she was excited.

She would be so mad if I moved away. I imagined her pounding her fists on the bed beside me. "You cannot go away!" she would say in a sharp, high voice. And then, we both would hug each other and burst into tears.

My pillow was getting soggy. I sat up and blew my nose.

At lunchtime, Mom's manager called Dad to say there were three tickets available for the Plummers and Ms. Morgan. "Their seats are farther back than ours," Dad said, "but I don't think anyone will mind."

That's fine, I thought. If they're in back, I won't have to watch Claire and Ms. Morgan together.

That afternoon, the doorbell rang. "Can I come in?" Claire asked.

A few minutes later, we sat on my bed. Claire opened a blue tote bag and pulled out yarn and knitting needles.

"What are you doing?" I asked.

She held up the blue yarn. "I'm making a cute headband for me. If it turns out nice, I'll make one like it for Ms. Morgan. We can wear them when we're a mother and daughter."

I kicked my heels against the side of the bed and looked at Mom's poster. I pictured her coming to life. She would say, "Katie needs a mother, too." No, she wouldn't. She would say, "Poor Claire. She needs a mother most of all."

"What are you thinking about?" Claire looked up from her needles. "You have a weird look on your face."

I straightened my face. "Nothing," I said.

Claire turned to look at Mom's poster, too. "Will she look like that? On Thursday?"

"Probably."

Claire's blue eyes stared at me. "You don't know?"

"Her concerts are always too far away. I've never gone to one."

"If my mother was a famous singer," Claire said, "I'd go see her all the time."

I jumped off my bed and pushed the button on my CD player. "I know the songs she'll sing."

Mom's voice came out of the speakers, singing about a train and saying good-bye. We listened to the whole thing.

Claire put down her knitting and clasped her hands together. "She wants to be at home, Katie. She's a very lonely person."

I frowned at her. "She was singing a sad song, that's all. She's been a singer since forever—since she was a teenager. She loves it."

"What are you going to wear to the concert?"

I pointed to my dresser drawers and shrugged.

"You should get your hair cut," Claire continued. "And make sure your teeth are very clean. If she likes you enough, she'll come back."

"Let's do something else," I said. I slid off the bed.

As we walked into the family room, Claire noticed the piles of stuff. "What are you doing with these things?"

"We're giving them away."

"How come?"

"I have to tell you something, Claire." I turned to face her. "We might move to Portland." I waved my hand at the piles. "Dad says we have to get rid of stuff so the house will look bigger. In case we need to sell it."

"You might move to Portland?" Claire's blue eyes got round.

"Yes."

Claire looked down at the floor. She was very still for a moment. At last, she spoke. "I don't want someone else to live in this house, Katie. Please don't move away."

I stared at her, surprised. She sounded like someone who liked me. My eyes filled with tears.

She kept looking at the floor, pushing her foot around on the carpet like she was drawing something.

"I don't want to go," I said, blinking back my tears. "But we might have to."

"Everything is sad here," she said. "I'm going home."

I watched Claire walk across the street with her tote bag under her arm. I envied Claire Plummer. She would keep on living in her house across the street. Ms. Morgan would be her new mother. I wondered if they would ever look over and remember Katie Jordan, that sad girl who used to live here.

Chapter 17

The Other Side of Giving Things Away

On Wednesday, Dad said we had enough things to take to the thrift shop. He was happier with me now because I had put more clothes in my pile. Mostly, they were fancy dresses that I had never worn. Mom never remembered that I didn't like ruffles. Or pink.

"Giving things to people who can use them is good for us," he said. "We should make a habit of doing this."

"I didn't like these anyway," I said.

He frowned at me.

We parked next to a sign that said "Donations Here" and carried our stuff through a door that rang a little bell every time we went through it. Three women were inside, taking clothes out of plastic bags and hanging them on hangers. "Thank you for bringing things in," one of the women said.

"I'll put these right out in the store," another one said. She gathered up our toys and carried them into another room. When the deck of Old Maid cards fell off the top, I picked it up and followed her.

People filled the aisles as they shopped for clothes and kitchen things. Next to the toy section was a corner filled with cute baby clothes. Kids were playing with some of the toys, and a girl my age was rocking a stroller with a sleeping baby in it while her mother picked out a tiny sundress.

Back in the sorting room, the women were gathered around a man who stood there holding a leash. A pretty yellow dog sat beside him.

"We hardly ever get a donated dog!" one woman said.

"The Humane Society will be here in a few minutes," the man said, patting the dog's head. It looked up at him with laughing eyes. "I hate to give her up," he said. "But the price of dog food . . ."

Dad was bringing in our last load. "Nice dog," he said and held out his hand. The dog sniffed his hand and then licked it. "A very nice dog," Dad said. He crouched down and rubbed the dog's shoulders and back. He looked up at the man. "You have to give her away?"

"I'm moving to San Diego," the man said in a soft voice. "My new place doesn't allow dogs. And like I say, it's expensive to feed her."

I knelt on the floor, and the dog came closer. First, she leaned against me. Then she sat down in my lap. "You're kinda big for this," I said feeling squished, but warm. I pushed my fingers through her hair and made it stand up in a ridge. Then I smoothed it back down. She wagged her tail.

"Lucy likes you." The man looked very sad.

"If I had this dog," I said, touching her nose with soft fingers, "I would brush her every day."

"We came to give things away," Dad said, "not to get things."

"I would feed her. Take her for walks. Give her a bath."

Dad turned to the man. "We might be moving, too. To Portland." He shook the man's hand. "Good luck with your dog."

One of the women touched my shoulder. "The Humane Society," she said, "will make sure she goes to a good home."

"But look at her face. She's very worried." I threw my arms around her again, and she licked my cheek with a long, wet tongue that smelled like dog food. She panted softly in my ear.

"Me, too." Tyler reached out to pat the top of Lucy's head.

"Say good-bye to Lucy," Dad said. "We have to go now."

Lucy's dark brown eyes looked up at Dad. I looked up at Dad, too.

"Absolutely not a good time to get a dog," Dad said. He reached down to scratch Lucy behind the ears. She thumped her back foot and smiled.

"She smiles," I said. "Oh my gosh. This dog smiles."

"Smile, dog," Tyler said. He moved closer to Lucy and peered into her mouth.

"Hello, there," a man said as he stepped around the bags of donations. "Someone called the Humane Society. Why, hello, pup." A tall man with hair as red as Tyler's held out his freckled hand. Lucy sniffed at it and then licked his fingers. "This one will be adopted in no time," the man said. "People like yellow labs."

"Dad," I said.

The man looked at us. "You folks want to be first on the waiting list?" he asked. "We need a few days to make sure the dog is healthy. When we put her up for adoption, we could call you first."

As Dad scratched Lucy's head again, I stopped breathing. I looked at Tyler. He wasn't breathing, either.

Even Lucy wasn't breathing. She stared up at Dad as if she knew her future was in his hands.

Dad rubbed his chin and closed his eyes. "Okay," he said with a sigh. "Please put us at the top of the list."

Lucy wagged her tail. Her dark eyes sparkled at us. She knew what Dad had said! She knew how much we wanted her.

We rubbed her and talked to her for a long time. Her owner showed us her tricks. She could sit and lie down and wait. She could even roll over! Finally, the man with the red hair put her in his car.

"Now," I said, as we got back into our car, "we have another reason not to move." Outside the car window, a girl my age walked past, carrying a familiar pink dress with ruffles. Dad saw her, too. He grinned at me.

I watched the girl get into a car and lay the dress carefully beside her on the seat. She patted the ruffles with soft fingers.

"Look at that," I said. "Cool!"

Chapter 18

Mom's Big Concert

Finally, Thursday came. Dad made Tyler take a long nap that afternoon. Then we packed some supper sandwiches and climbed into the car.

"It will take an hour and a half to get to Portland," Dad said as he waited for me to get buckled in. "Don't keep asking me if we're there yet."

While we ate our tuna sandwiches, I watched boring traffic. All these cars going to Portland, I thought. All these people driving along beside us. Were they glad to be going there? Didn't they wish they could live in Hartsdale like us?

"I wish we had taken a picture of Lucy," I said to the back of Dad's head. "We could have showed Mom our new dog."

"She is not our new dog." Dad checked for traffic and pulled out to pass. "You can't get a new dog and then pack up and move. It's too confusing. You can't do that to a dog."

"If the dog really loved us," I said, "and we really loved the dog, it would be okay, wouldn't it?"

He clicked off his turn signal and closed his hands around the steering wheel. He didn't answer.

I thought about Mom. Would she hold the microphone in her hand like a famous star? Would she sing my favorite songs? Would there be lots of people?

What about after the concert, when Tyler would ask her to come home? Would she say, "Yes, but I thought you didn't want me anymore"? And then, we would all cry and be happy.

I stared at the back of Dad's head. Would he be glad if Mom said yes? I thought so. His face sometimes looked like Tyler's when he talked about Mom.

Beside me in the back seat, Tyler pretended to read a picture book to the stuffed animals he had brought. He made his animals act out the stories.

"Are you my mother?" his stuffed duck quacked. The teddy bear answered in a growly voice, "No, my dear one. I am not your mother."

"Then, boo-hoo, I'll keep looking," quacked the little duck.

"Tyler can't take his stuffed animals into the concert," I said to Dad. "Can he?"

"That's right," Dad said. "Stuffed animals stay in the car."

"Hear that, Tyler?" I asked.

Tyler made the duck nod at me, and then he kept on playing.

"Are we going to be late?" I asked. The clock on the dashboard said 7:15. "Doesn't the concert start at 7:30?"

"We might be late," Dad said.

"Why are we always late?" I asked. Would Mom wave and say hi to us from up on the stage?

Would she be so excited she'd run down to give us hugs?

"We're not always late," Dad said.

A few minutes later, we reached the waterfront park and drove around looking for a place to leave the car. "I always forget how busy things are in Portland," Dad said.

Portland, I thought. Where I might live. One side of the car windows was filled with tall buildings that leaned against each other. On the other side, there was a huge park and the river. The same river ran through Hartsdale, but here the river bustled with big boats. Bridges criss-crossed over it. Cars zoomed everywhere. I sighed. In Portland, everybody was in a hurry.

"Read to me," Tyler said. "Read the one about the baby duck looking for its mother."

"I can't," I told him. "We're almost there."

Right then, Dad found a parking place. As soon as he stopped the car, we jumped out and ran toward a big white tent. "You're fine," the ticket man said. "They're starting late."

Dad pointed to a building marked RESTROOMS. "Need to go?" he asked us.

Tyler and I shook our heads.

Inside the tent, people were crowded together, sitting in rows of folding chairs. Ahead of us, the brightly lit stage held a set of drums and microphones and guitars. Close to the stage, Dad found three seats that had been saved just for us.

She didn't forget we were coming, I thought.

"Excuse us," Dad said, as we pushed past people's knees.

The announcer walked out while we got settled in our seats. "Howdy, folks," he shouted as everyone whistled and cheered and clapped. "Tonight," he shouted, "we're lucky to have one of the finest country singers in the world. Please welcome," he stopped to take a breath, "Roxanne Winter!"

The whistles and cheers started up again. I grabbed Dad's hand as excitement leaped through my arms and legs. For a long moment, nothing happened. Then Mom came running out—her hair shiny and big. Her white jeans and high white boots glowed in the stage lights. Her red shirt flashed with sequins.

I drew in my breath. Was that really Mom? So beautiful?

Dad grinned down at me and squeezed my hand. "That's her," he said.

"Mommy," Tyler yelled. But she couldn't hear him; the crowd was too loud. Mom moved to the microphone. "Hi, everybody," she said, but people kept on cheering. When at last they quieted down, she looked right at us. "I want to say a special hello to my favorite people who are here tonight."

I grinned back at her, wanting to jump up on that stage and fly into her arms. I clapped my hands to my cheeks so they wouldn't burst.

Mom nodded to the band members who were standing behind her. She strummed a few chords on her guitar, and when she began to sing, everyone sat very still. Mom's voice filled me up with happiness and pride. Watching her face as she sang each line was a hundred times better than listening to her CDs. She was singing to everyone, but especially to Dad and Tyler and me.

I looked up at Dad, but he was smiling at Mom. I looked closer at his eyes. They were shiny like he might be crying. Just then, Tyler stood up on his chair and started to jump.

"Dad," I said, but he couldn't hear me, so I grabbed his hand and pointed at Tyler.

Dad blinked his eyes and reached for Tyler. "Sit here," he said, and gathered him into his lap.

The first half of the concert flew by like a dream. After every song, the people yelled and clapped until my ears hurt.

"We'll be back after a short intermission," Mom said. She waved and blew kisses at the audience. At us. At me! Then she walked off the stage.

Chapter 19

Claire's Terrible News

My ears still thumped with the sounds of the bass and the guitars as people got up and stretched. We moved along with them to a place where there were tables set up for selling T-shirts and CDs. Claire and Ms. Morgan stood near one of the tables. I showed Dad where I was going and pushed through the crowd.

Claire grabbed me. "Your mother is so pretty," she said. "She acts really famous."

I nodded and coughed. My voice wasn't working very well.

Claire came closer so I could hear her over all the noise. "Do you like my new clothes?" She smoothed her jeans jacket and held up one foot so I could see her blue leather boots. "My favorite thing is this hat," she said, adjusting it over her blond curls. "It's so perfect." She turned in a slow circle in front of me.

"You look like a cowgirl," I said.

"Ms. Morgan said that, too." She bent close to whisper in my ear. "But something terrible has happened. Ms. Morgan is having a barbecue for all of us tomorrow."

"That's not terrible."

"Yes, it is. Tell you later." Claire pressed her lips together as Ms. Morgan finished paying for her CDs and moved with us away from the table.

"It's a wonderful concert," Ms. Morgan said to me.

Mr. Plummer came up with plastic bottles of water. "That's quite a mother you have," he said. "I'm enjoying this." He handed Claire and Ms. Morgan their bottles.

"Where are your dad and Tyler?" Ms. Morgan asked. "Oh, there they are." Ms. Morgan waved at Dad, who was working his way toward us through the crowd while I wondered what the terrible thing could be. I looked at Claire, but she just shook her head.

"I'm so glad you found us among all these people," Ms. Morgan said to Dad. "I want to invite you all to my barbecue. Tomorrow afternoon. Very short notice, but I have a special person coming to visit. I'd like you all to meet him."

"See?" Claire pulled me to one side and breathed into my ear. "She . . . has . . . a . . . boyfriend!" She pushed her hands into her jacket pockets and turned away.

I looked at Ms. Morgan. She would never be Claire's mother. Or mine. She was taken.

"We'd love to come," Dad said to Ms. Morgan. "We'll need your address."

As Dad wrote down her address, she bent close to him. "She is beautiful, Bill," she said. "Is this hard for you?"

I watched Dad nod at her. His eyes blinked behind his glasses, and then he looked out over the crowd as he tucked the paper into his pocket.

Ms. Morgan touched Dad's hand. "The three of you are a good family, you know. Your children are lucky they have you for a dad."

I leaned against Dad, proud of him.

"Tyler and Katie still miss her a lot," Dad said. "Seeing her tonight is bitter and sweet for all of us."

"Bittersweet," Ms. Morgan said. "I understand."

I moved closer to ask how something could be bitter and sweet all at the same time, but Dad cleared his throat and looked over at Mr. Plummer's cowboy hat. "Did you and Claire just fly in from Texas?"

Claire and Mr. Plummer smiled. They both reached up to straighten their hats.

"You're all blue," Tyler said. "You should have a red jacket like mine."

Dad shook his head at Tyler. "That's not polite." He turned to Ms. Morgan. "Thanks, Janna, for telling me about that thrift shop. We went there yesterday."

"We found a dog," I said, suddenly remembering.

"She's maybe going to be our dog!" Tyler said. "She knows how to smile!"

"Wow," Ms. Morgan said. "A dog that smiles. I can't wait to see her."

"Dogs are messy," Claire said, rolling her eyes. "And they leave you-know-what all over the place. Dog hair, too."

"She's pretty sweet," Dad said. "A yellow lab. The trouble is," but as he started to tell them we might not be able to get the dog, some bells rang and lights went off and on.

"That means the second half is starting," Mr. Plummer said. We turned and moved with all the people who were going back to their seats.

Mr. Plummer pulled an envelope out of his pocket and handed it to Dad. "I printed out some photos of our picnic. These are for you."

"Thanks," Dad said. He hustled us down the aisle, and we sat down, ready to hear Mom sing again.

I looked up at the microphone she would soon

hold in her hand and felt excitement bubble again in my stomach. Mom is so wonderful, I thought. Beside me a man began to clap his hands together. "Roxanne," he yelled.

I moved closer to Dad. I wasn't sure I liked sharing Mom with all these people I didn't know. Maybe that was what Dad meant by bitter and sweet.

Chapter 20

Tyler: Lost!

I curled my legs under me and settled in, but before Mom had finished the first song, Tyler was pulling on my sleeve. "I have to go," he said, his face wrinkled with worry. "Right now."

Dad sighed. "I just took you," he whispered.

"I have to go, too," I said. "I forgot to go at intermission. I'll take him."

"Are you sure you know where?" Dad looked out at the aisle and all the people we would have to crawl past.

"That building right near the door. It's easy." While the audience was clapping for Mom's song, I led Tyler up the aisle and out the front of the tent. "I'm here, too," Dad said, coming up behind us. "I'll wait by the door."

“Come on,” I told Tyler as I pulled him toward the women’s end.

He stopped and twisted the sleeve of his red jacket out of my hand. “I’m going there,” he said, pointing to the men’s door.

“You can’t. You have to stay with me.” I hustled him into the building and into a stall. I ran into the stall next to his.

When I was done, I washed my hands and looked at Tyler’s stall. “I’m going outside so I can hear better. Hurry up.”

He didn’t answer.

A moment later, I leaned against Dad by the door of the big tent and listened to Mom. She was singing the song about the train. From out here, she sounded exactly like her CD.

“Is Tyler coming?” Dad asked.

“He’s coming.” I leaned harder against Dad. “What did that mean,” I asked him, “what you said to Ms. Morgan? About bittersweet?”

He bent close to my ear and spoke softly. “Something that’s bittersweet is happy and sad all at the same time. It means it’s great to see your mom again." He stopped and then went on. "But we can also see that her life is different now."

"She won't ever come back." My voice sounded grown up. And sad.

He nodded. "That's the part that is bitter. She's done very well, and since we love her, we have to be happy for her. That part is sweet."

I leaned harder against Dad. "Tyler thinks she'll come home with us."

"I wish he didn't miss her so much." Dad shifted his feet and looked toward the restroom. He took my hand and rubbed it against his chest. "The three of us make a good family."

Inside the tent, the crowd clapped and cheered again. The bass player was talking now about some place they had traveled to before Portland.

Dad smiled down at me. "We three are stuck together, you know." He looked again at the restrooms. "Go check," he said. "He's taking too long."

In the ladies' room, Tyler's stall was wide open, and no one was there. How had he gotten past us? I ran back outside.

Dad ran to meet me. "Where is he?"

"Is there a problem?" a voice asked. It was one of the people who sold CDs.

"My son," Dad said, his voice rough. "He's wearing a red jacket."

"I think I saw him go back into the concert," the man said.

I took a deep breath. That was it, of course.

Dad and I rushed down the aisle. Up by the stage, bunches of people were dancing to the music. They all wore cowboy hats and boots.

The people who weren't dancing were clapping and stomping their feet. We stopped at the end of our row, looking down it for Tyler. Our three seats stood empty. "He's gone," I shouted over the music and the clapping. "Tyler is gone."

I burst into tears as Dad grabbed my hand and rushed back up the aisle. "Excuse me, excuse me," he said to the people who were dancing in the aisle. The music ended, and people began to cheer and clap.

I panted, trying to keep up with Dad's long legs.

All at once, the clapping around us grew choppy and finally stopped. Someone laughed. Then another person laughed. “Look at that cute kid,” someone said.

Cute kid?

Dad stopped running, and I bumped into his back. We both turned to look at the stage.

Mom was telling the audience about her next song. Behind her was a little boy wearing a red jacket.

Chapter 21

The Biggest Question

Dad and I stood without breathing, watching Tyler up there on the big stage. Tyler lifted his hand to shade his eyes from the bright lights and walked toward Mom. Still holding the microphone, she turned around to see what everyone else could see.

"We have a visitor," the drummer said. He played a drum roll and the crowd laughed.

"Tyler?" Mom's voice all at once sounded more like Mom than it had all night.

Dad took my hand. "Thank God," he said. "He's okay."

"Should we get him?"

"In a minute." Dad hunkered down in the aisle and pulled me close.

Mom handed her guitar to the bass player and slid the mike into its holder. "Come see me," she said, her voice softer, but still being picked up by the mikes. She held out her arms.

Tyler stood still, peeking through his fingers at Mom. "It's hard to see," his little voice said.

Mom went to him and pulled him into her arms. "I've got you now." She turned to the audience and smiled. The crowd burst into applause.

"We have to keep the songs coming along," Mom said to Tyler. "Will you sing one with me?" He stuck his thumb into his mouth and shook his head.

"Down in the valley," she sang into the mike, and then she waved to the audience to join in.

"Valley so low," the crowd sang.

In Mom's arms, Tyler raised his head and pulled his thumb out of his mouth. Of course, he could sing the tucking-into-bed song. "Hang your head over." Tyler's voice came through the mike loud and clear. "Hear the wind blow."

Dad rubbed his cheeks against his sleeve. Then he blew his nose and grinned a crooked grin at me. "That kid," he said, shaking his head.

By the time "Down in the Valley" ended, the people around us were mopping their eyes and blowing their noses. They clapped, and Mom set Tyler down on his feet. She took his hand, and they both bowed. "That's my boy," Mom said. The crowd roared.

She shaded her eyes and looked out. "Is your dad out there? And Katie?"

Dad and I ran down the aisle to the stage. "Tyler," Dad said. "Come sit with us now."

But Tyler shook his head. "I have to ask Mommy the biggest question," he said, and once again, the mikes picked up his voice.

"Not now," Dad said. "Ask her later."

"Mommy," Tyler said, and his voice rang through the speakers. "You've been gone too long. Katie and I want you to come back to live with us. Will you?"

Katie and I want you to come back to live with us! The words echoed around the big tent. The crowd grew silent. Everyone waited for Mom's answer.

She held her hand over her eyes, shading them from the lights. Finally she saw Dad and me and gave us a little wave. She gathered Tyler into her arms and whispered something in his ear.

He nodded. "I love you, too," he said.

She set him on his feet and gave him a gentle push in our direction. Once Dad had lifted him off the stage, she reached for her guitar and moved to the main mike. "This is for every person . . ." she said. Then, she coughed and cleared her throat. "For every person, who for some reason, cannot go back."

The band swung into action and suddenly they were playing a familiar song. Mom stepped to the mike, and her voice came out sweet and quiet. “Where is the place where all my dreams start?” she sang. “Where is the home that lives in my heart?”

Dad picked Tyler up, and a moment later, we were sitting again in our seats.

Chapter 22

The Answer

Tyler crawled into Dad's lap. "I don't think she's coming," he said.

"It was okay to ask," Dad said in a husky voice.

I leaned against Dad's arm. We were three people stuck together in this huge crowd of people who loved Mom. And Mom? Who did she love?

I knew the answer to that. She loved Tyler and me and Dad. But she loved being a star more.

Dad's arm felt good against mine. I grabbed it and pulled it around me.

Bittersweet. I knew exactly what that meant.

Chapter 23

Pizza with Mom

Mom did the rest of her show—fast songs and slow songs, and songs that everyone sang along with her. At the end, people cheered and yelled until she did two more songs. Finally, she waved good-bye and left the stage. The lights came on. Everyone stood up, and I did, too, blinking and exhausted.

Dad looked at his watch as we shuffled along with all the people. "Wow. It's late. She wants us to have supper with her." He picked up Tyler and took my hand. We moved through the lines of people toward a side door of the tent.

"Tyler's not going to eat anything," I said. His head bounced on Dad's shoulder; his eyes drooped.

A man met us at the side door and led us through the fresh, cool air toward a huge black-and-gold RV. "Is this Mom's?" I shivered. She really was a star.

Dad knocked on the door. "This is how she lives now that she's performing so much. It's more comfortable than finding a motel every night."

This is Mom's real home, I thought. Her house has wheels, but it's her home just the same.

Standing at the door was the bass player, looking like somebody's grandpa. His shoulders drooped, and he looked tired. He waved us inside, where there was a whole living room and a kitchen. "She's taking off the make-up," he said in a soft, rough voice.

"I'll be right out," Mom yelled from somewhere down the hall.

"So here's the newest member of the band," the bass player said to Tyler. Tyler raised his head and blinked.

Mom came in, wearing a soft green robe and slippers. "Feels so good to get that stuff off my face," she said. "And those boots off my feet."

"See ya later, Roxie," the bass player said. He went out the door.

"Oh, he's gone," Mom said, "I was going to introduce all of you to him. Guess he figured out who you were." She reached out to me, and I stepped into her hug. "Did you like the show, honey?"

"You were great, Mom," I said, breathing in clouds of perfume, feeling her arms warm around me.

"Hey there, Tyler," she said with a grin as Dad handed him over to her. "The big star of my show."

"Hi, Mommy," Tyler said. He wrapped his arms around her neck and gave her a wet kiss.

"I'm sorry that happened, Roxie," Dad said. "I hope it didn't mess things up."

"It didn't." She stopped then. "Well, it changed the timing. But it worked out fine. Right?"

There was silence before Dad nodded.

"Right," he said.

Mom sat down at a little table that had couches around it. "Pizza is coming." She patted the couch and smiled as we crowded in. "So tell me," she said, "what did you really think of the show?"

"Your voice is better than ever," Dad said. "You look great, Roxie."

She smoothed her hair. "I don't look too tired? This extra show has been a big problem. We have to be in Spokane tomorrow night. What is that, a six-hour drive?"

I studied Mom's face. She didn't look tired at all. She looked excited.

She turned to me. "I'm glad you're here," she said. "Don't you have school tomorrow?"

"It's summer vacation," I said, surprised that she didn't know. "No school."

"We'll sleep in," Dad said.

Tyler wiggled on the couch and leaned against Mom. "Not me," he said.

"Oh, that's right." Dad sighed. "The early riser."

Mom made a face. "After a concert, I sleep till noon." She got up and opened the refrigerator. "Want something to drink?" She set bottled water on the table, along with a couple of Cokes.

"Uh," Dad said, "no caffeine for the kids, Roxie."

"Right," she said. "I forgot." She put the Cokes back and got out some juice.

Just then, someone knocked on the door. "Oh dear," Mom said. "The pizza. I can't answer looking like this." She backed away from the door, down the hall, out of sight.

"I'll get it," Dad said. He opened the door to the smell of pizza.

"He's going to need money," Mom called from the hallway.

Dad reached for his wallet. "I'll treat." He gave the pizza man some bills and closed the door.

"Oh, Bill," Mom said, coming back to the table. "You didn't have to treat. But thank you." She opened the lid of the box and peeked inside. "Yummy!"

I looked inside the box, too.

Mom had forgotten! I hate mushrooms!

Chapter 24

Good-bye Again

Horrible mushrooms covered every bit of the pizza. "Mom!" I said as tears rushed into my eyes.

Dad shook his head at me and reached for a piece. I pressed my lips together and watched him pick off mushrooms. He slid my piece over to me.

"Oh, Katie," Mom said. "Guess I forgot."

"It's okay." I blinked the tears away and tried to smile.

"You've grown since Christmas, Katie," she said, pulling me closer to her.

I rubbed my cheek against her soft robe, trying to forget about the mushrooms. "This bus is cute," I said. "I like these little cabinets and shelves."

"Look up there." She pointed behind me, and I twisted around to look.

"Our pictures!"

"I keep the Scotch tape handy. Everything you send me goes up on the wall." Mom nodded at me. "Makes this rig feel like a home."

"We'll send more," I said. "I do birds now." I looked down at my pizza. Dad had missed a lot of mushrooms. They were still everywhere.

Mom got up for another bottle of water. "It's summer vacation, huh? What have you been doing?"

"We've hardly had a chance to play," I told her. "Dad's been making us sort stuff."

"We're giving away extra things," Dad said, "in case I take a job in Portland."

"You would love it here in Portland," Mom said. "There's so much going on." Outside the rig, a siren whistled, coming closer and then finally turning away from us.

I started to say, no, we wouldn't, but Tyler interrupted.

"We went on a picnic," he said, sitting up and opening his eyes. "With the Plummers and Ms. Morgan."

"Silver Creek Falls," Dad said. He wiped tomato sauce off Tyler's mouth.

"We went there," Mom said. "Oh my gosh. Was Tyler even born yet?"

"Katie was a baby." He pulled the envelope from his pocket. "Want to see some photos?"

Mom wiped pizza off her fingers and took the first photo. "Is that little Claire Plummer?" she asked. "I can't believe it."

"Little Claire Plummer is quite the little lady now." Dad grinned at me.

"She's mostly a pain," I said.

"Isn't she the one who helped you take care of pets over spring vacation?" Mom asked.

I nodded. "Sometimes she's okay. She told me she was sad we might move."

"Who is this pretty woman?" Mom put her finger on Ms. Morgan.

"My teacher," I told her. "She's wonderful."

"Katie's teacher," Tyler said with a yawn, "is very wonderful." He propped his head up with one hand, and his eyes drooped again.

Mom hugged Tyler closer to her. "She must be seriously dating Claire's dad. Look at the three of them."

I took the photo from Mom and stared at Ms. Morgan and Claire and Mr. Plummer sitting side by side on the picnic bench. "We just found out she has a boyfriend," I said, but Mom had turned to the next picture, one of Tyler and Dad and me ducking under a waterfall.

When Tyler put his head in Mom's lap and fell asleep, Dad looked at his watch.

"Don't go yet," Mom said. "I need to make sure you all understand about . . . about why I can't come home."

"Seeing you perform tonight made it really clear," Dad said. "You're a professional."

I nodded as I remembered the cheers, the clapping, the excitement.

She looked down at Tyler and brushed his red

hair back from his forehead. "I miss you all very much," she said in a soft voice.

"But," I asked, already knowing the answer, "you don't want to do mom things anymore?"

"I'll always be your mom. But I don't have time to be the kind of mom who lives at home with you." She shook her head slowly back and forth. "I'm sorry, Katie."

I looked away from her. "You would probably have trouble," I said, "getting up early for Tyler. And cooking for us."

"Cooking is not my strong point," Mom said.

I folded my mushroomy pizza into my paper napkin and pushed it away from me along with dreams of Mom bringing pancakes to the table or baking cookies. This is one of those bitter times, I thought, but a moment later, I remembered the sweet parts. "Singing makes you really happy, Mom. We'll be okay."

Dad nodded. "Katie and I talked about it tonight. We really are okay."

Mom blotted her eyes with a paper napkin. She turned then and looked at the big calendar that hung on the side of the refrigerator. "August is coming. We'll have our time together."

"The last two weeks of August," Dad said.

I nodded. "At Grandma's house."

"Your grandma is coming to my Spokane concert tomorrow," Mom said, starting to smile again. "She's bringing her whole bridge group to the concert." She hummed and sang, "You've got to know when to hold'em, know when to fold'em." She laughed. "I'll sing them a card-playing song."

"Mom," I said, "I know how to play Crazy Eights now. Can we play when we visit you?"

"Definitely. We'll play Crazy Eights every day."

Tyler sat up and rubbed his eyes. "We might bring a dog," he said.

"A dog?"

"Lucy," I said, "is the most wonderful dog." I hugged my arms around myself and remembered Lucy's warm, soft fur and her dark eyes.

"She smiles." Tyler was suddenly wide awake. "Like this." He pulled his lips into a big grin.

"She wags her tail all over the place. It's this long, her tail." I lifted my arms to show Mom.

"We're not sure yet about the dog." Dad got up and walked toward the door. "Right now, we need to get on the road."

Mom hugged Dad. Then she pulled open a cabinet door. "I have some T-shirts for Katie and Tyler. And some new CDs."

She hugged Tyler and then me. "I really do miss you all," she said. She bit her lip and looked at Dad. I could see tears in her eyes.

"We miss you, too, Mom," I said. Her strong arms kept on holding me close while her perfume floated around me.

"We'll have a great time in August," she said in a husky voice. As we went down the steps and started across the park, she stood in the door of the RV and waved good-bye.

A few minutes later, we got into our car. Pretty soon, we were back on the freeway, headed for home. After a while, I saw Dad looking into the mirror at me in the back seat. "You guys okay back there?"

"Sure," I said, thinking he wanted to be sure my seat belt was fastened all the way. Then, I thought, maybe he was talking about the bittersweet. "I'm fine, Dad," I told him, but as I curled up on the seat to sleep, I could feel a big empty place inside me.

Chapter 25

Now What?

Mom was in my dreams all night. First she sang. Then she held me close, and I saw tears come into her eyes. In my last dream, she held out a piece of pizza. "No mushrooms," she said.

When I woke up, I looked at her poster. She was probably on her way to Spokane right now. Maybe she was looking out the RV window and thinking about August and how we would be together.

She was probably thinking about the next concert. She was probably practicing the card-playing song.

In the kitchen, I poured myself some Cheerios and sat down at the table with Dad. "There's one good thing today. Ms. Morgan's barbecue."

"Right," Dad said.

I sat up straight, remembering. "Did you hear about her boyfriend? That's why she's having the barbecue."

"I heard that," he said, cranking his head around to loosen his neck.

"Claire's really sad that Ms. Morgan can't be her new mother."

He was quiet. "Today is the day," he finally said, "when SolaCom said they would call me back about a possible job."

Solacom. It didn't even sound nice.

He sipped his coffee and set the mug down. "If they want me, I'll tell them I'll think about it. I have to talk with Mr. Flagstaff first."

I sighed and pushed my spoon through my cereal.

"He'll be back on Tuesday," Dad said.

"Tuesday is years from now." I took a big mouthful of cereal and chewed it. Swallowed.

"Maybe we can get Lucy today."

"That man said he'd call. They have to make sure she's healthy."

I stared into my bowl of cereal, and all the little circles blurred together. "She's worried. She's wondering why we haven't come to get her. She doesn't have any family right now."

Tyler dragged into the family room with his blanket around him. He curled into a chair at the table. Dad brought him a bowl of cereal.

Tyler picked up his spoon and right away dropped it on the floor. "My spoon," he wailed. His eyes filled with tears.

"Uh-oh," Dad said, getting him another spoon. "This is going to be a long day. For more than one reason."

I thunked my own spoon on the table. "Nothing is ever settled," I said. "I want Sierra to come back so we can do stuff before we move away. This summer vacation is the dumbest one I've ever had."

Dad nodded at me. "It's hard on all of us."

"We could settle one thing," I said. "We could

decide about getting Lucy right now."

Dad got up and went to the kitchen to pour more coffee. He didn't answer.

I watched Tyler loading his new spoon with Cheerios. He put one more on the top of the heap and opened his mouth. I looked away.

When the phone rang, Dad handed it to me.

"I cried all night," Claire said, "because Ms. Morgan has a boyfriend. She'll never be my mother."

Or mine, I thought. But then, as usual, I thought of Mom. But today I knew for sure that Mom was never coming back. "Things are awful here, too," I told her. "Everything was simpler when we were in fourth grade."

I could tell she was nodding at the other end of the phone. "Anyway," she said, "I'm writing songs for your mom to sing."

"For Mom?"

I'll need you to send them to her, okay? She's going to love them. She'll probably pay me."

I slid down to the floor and rested my head on my hand.

"I'll sing you one right now," Claire said. She began to sing and right away stopped. "I've lost the note," she said. "I have to go find it on the piano." She hung up.

In the utility room, Dad was flattening cardboard boxes.

"We can use some of these for moving," he said.

"Wait!" I yelled as he reached for the next box. "Stop! I need that one!"

"I'm making space in here," he said. "This box is too big for anything anyway."

"I want it," I said. Tears flew into my eyes. "Please, Dad?"

He looked at me. "Why?" he asked, pushing it toward me.

I stepped into it and curled myself into a ball. "It's perfect." I stuck my head up to look out at him. "When Lucy comes. . ."

He shook his head at me.

"If. If Lucy comes, this will be her bed. If we move, she won't be a bit worried because her bed will go everywhere we go."

He heaved a big sigh.

"Please, Dad?"

He shook his head again. "You can play with the box. I won't flatten it yet."

"Now," I told him, "all she needs is a really nice blanket. Some toys. A pretty dish for water. . ."

Chapter 26

Ms. Morgan's Barbeque

"You found the right place," someone called, and there was Ms. Morgan, coming down from her front porch to meet us. "Welcome," she said, and her green eyes sparkled at us. She scooped Tyler up for a hug. "You were so brave on that big stage!"

"Mommy says I'm in her band now," he said, "but I don't think so."

"How is everyone doing?" she asked Dad.

"Okay, I think," he said. "Tyler took a good nap this afternoon."

He didn't mention that Tyler napped on his blanket in Lucy's cardboard box. We were going to have a big problem, Tyler and I, deciding which room Lucy would sleep in. If we got her.

Ms. Morgan let Tyler slide down and held his hand as we walked up the steps. "Did you get your phone call?"

Dad shook his head. "They'll probably call on Monday."

"I'm interested," she said. "Let me know what happens."

I had forgotten all about Dad expecting the solar company to call. He didn't look upset. He was sure better at waiting than me.

"The backyard is a mess," Ms. Morgan said, leading us into her house. "My backpacking tent came. I'm trying to set it up. I didn't know it would have so many pieces."

Ms. Morgan's house smelled like apple pie. We walked through her living room that had books piled everywhere.

The backyard had red flowers along the fence. Yummy chicken smells came from the barbecue.

At the other end of the yard, I saw tent poles and bags and a little orange tent with a sagging top.

I looked around for her boyfriend. No one else was here.

"Good idea to set up a new tent before you go," Dad said. "Sometimes, they leave out an important part."

"Can I go in?" Tyler peeked inside the tent.

"Take off your shoes." Ms. Morgan unzipped the door for him.

Tyler crawled inside and rolled onto his back. He smiled up at us. "I like it," he said.

"No rain in the forecast," Dad said

Ms. Morgan gasped. "I forgot about rain. Should I take a rain parka, too?" She waved her hand at the picnic table. "See this stuff? All of it is supposed to go into my backpack."

I looked at the clothes and cooking pots and a sleeping bag and a pad. "It's never going to fit."

She made a face. "I've got to take less." She grabbed a long fork off the table. "I'm not taking this in my backpack. It's for turning the chicken." We followed her to the grill.

"May I do it?" Dad asked, holding his hand out for the fork. "Where are you going to backpack?" he asked as he turned the chicken pieces.

"Mt. Jefferson Park," Ms. Morgan said.

"A beautiful trail," Dad said. A minute later, they had put the cover back on the grill and were bent over forest maps, discussing the trails.

In the tent, Tyler was singing a song about spruced-up trees. Ms. Morgan and Dad weren't paying any attention to me, but it didn't matter. I leaned back against the table and listened. This party felt cozy. If only Sierra were here, it would be perfect.

Nobody else heard the knocking on the front door.

Chapter 27

Unexpected Guests

When I went inside Ms. Morgan's house, Claire and Mr. Plummer stood on the front porch. "Please come in," I said, pretending I was Ms. Morgan.

Mr. Plummer moved some books on the coffee table so he could set down a vase of roses. "The Peace rose is in full bloom right now," he said. "I can bring some to your family, too, Katie."

"Thanks." I breathed in the heavenly rose smell.

When I straightened up, I saw Ms. Morgan's mantel. There, in the exact center, was the bluebird plate I had made. That bird looked right at home.

Claire pulled me away from the mantel. "Did you see him?" she asked.

"Him?"

"Her boyfriend." She frowned at me. "I already hate him."

"He's not here."

"Where is he?"

"I don't know."

They followed me through the house and out the back door. Soon we were all trying to make the tent stand up better.

Sometime later, I heard another knock on the door. Ms. Morgan was turning the chicken again, and the fathers were discussing tent stakes, so I went to the front door. This time it would be the boyfriend.

But no!

It was Mrs. Ramirez, the one who owned the bride shop, and Alex was with her. I stared at

Mrs. Ramirez. She was surely here to help Ms. Morgan plan her wedding to the boyfriend. They would be choosing dresses and stuff. They were going to ruin the barbecue.

"We live next door," Mrs. Ramirez said. "I think you and Alejandro know each other."

I stared at her a moment before I realized what she had said. They had also been invited to the barbecue. They were neighbors. That explained why Ms. Morgan and Alex biked to the library together.

Mrs. Ramirez had wound her long black hair into a fancy knot at the back of her head, and a soft blue scarf floated across her shoulders. "We brought tamales," she said. "I'll leave them here on the kitchen counter."

Alex had on his favorite shirt. "Hi, Katie." He shoved his hands into his pants pockets. He had to lift up the shirt flaps to do it.

"They're in the backyard," I said. "Ms. Morgan has a new tent."

"Cool." Alex followed his mother and me out the back door. Claire was sitting at the picnic table. When she saw Alex, she rolled her eyes. Then, she saw Alex's mother's blue scarf and her eyes lit up.

"I'm Claire Plummer," she said, and held out her hand to Mrs. Ramirez.

Mrs. Ramirez looked amazed. "I didn't know young people were brought up this way anymore," she said.

Dad grinned at me as he introduced himself. "See?" he said. "Manners are important." He winked at me and went back to the tent.

"I'm Tina Ramirez," Alex's mother said to Mr. Plummer. "Janna tells me we have much in common."

"Tina Ramirez," Mr. Plummer said. "Yes, we do. I'm an interior decorator. I've wondered many times who designs the windows of your store. They are very nicely done."

"I do it," Mrs. Ramirez said as she and Mr. Plummer settled on the picnic bench next to Claire. They began to talk about wedding fashions. "Come on, Alex," I said. "Let's look at the tent."

Tyler came running. "My library friend!" he yelled. "Did you bring your bridge book?"

"I can go next door and get it," Alex said. "First, I want to see the tent."

"Please take your shoes off before you go in," Ms. Morgan reminded us. "One person at a time."

Alex and Tyler and I took turns going in and out and lying flat on the floor of the tent, looking up through the mesh ceiling at the trees and the sky. We loved that tent.

"Now that everyone's here, I need to call Eric." Ms. Morgan looked at the back door and smiled. "There you are! I thought you were going to sleep forever."

Chapter 28

Little Brothers Grow Up?

A tall, dark-haired man came into the backyard.

"This is Eric," Ms. Morgan said, putting her arm around the man's waist.

He held his hand out for Dad to shake. "I've heard all about this family," he said with a grin. "The famous Katie," he said, "and the famous Tyler." As he turned to me, I saw his green eyes were just like Ms. Morgan's eyes.

All at once, I knew exactly who he was.

"Eric is my little brother," Ms. Morgan said. "He got in late last night from Seattle, so I let him take a nap. We're going backpacking together."

"Good to meet you," Dad said, shaking Eric's hand.

Claire looked up. "Brother?"

At that moment, Mrs. Ramirez's scarf slid off her shoulders. Claire jumped up. "Let me fix it for you," she said.

"Thank you. You have a sweet daughter," Mrs. Ramirez said, smiling at Mr. Plummer. She turned to Claire. "This would look nice on you." She tied the scarf around Claire's shoulders.

"I knew the three of you would hit it off," Ms. Morgan said to Claire. "The chicken is done," she said as she stuffed things quickly into her backpack. "We need this table for eating."

In the kitchen, we walked along the counters and spooned our plates full of tamales and baked beans and fruit salad. Then we went out to the grill where Eric served us the chicken.

"I had so much fun getting ready for this picnic," Ms. Morgan said as she sat down at the table. She looked all around the group. "This is my first big party here in Hartsdale. Thank you so much for coming."

"Five years between us," Eric was saying to Dad.

"The same as Katie and Tyler," Dad said.

"What's the same?" I asked.

"Age difference," Dad said. "Ms. Morgan is five years older than Eric."

I swallowed a bite of chicken and looked back and forth at the two of them. I had never thought that some day Tyler would get as tall as me. That he would grow up to be a man!

"We'll have to talk," Ms. Morgan said, winking at me, "about what it's like, having a little brother in the family."

"Don't tell every story," Eric begged. "Only tell her the good things."

"There are lots of good things," Ms. Morgan said, "but they're not as interesting as the bad things." She patted her brother's arm.

Across the table, Tyler smacked his lips and I saw a blob of macaroni and cheese fall down the front of his shirt. I shook my head. I couldn't imagine him growing up.

Tyler cleared his throat. "We might get a dog," he said to everyone.

"We had one while I was growing up," Ms. Morgan said. "I shared my dog biscuits with him." She laughed. "I was sure they were my biscuits. Not the dog's."

"Those were my biscuits," Eric said, spreading butter on a hard roll. He winked at me and pushed the butter plate toward Dad.

"The dog I had was a mutt," Dad said. "We answered an ad in the classifieds."

"I had a cat," Mr. Plummer said.

Claire stopped whooshing away a pesky fly and turned to stare at him. "How come we don't have a cat?"

"I thought you were going to get fish," I said. We told everyone about the fish we took care of during spring vacation.

Ms. Morgan poured more lemonade for Alex, Tyler, Claire, and me. "Did you see your paper plate picture?" she asked as she poured mine.

"I put it on the mantel. The place of honor."

"Katie is quite an artist," Dad said.

"Both your children are very special," Ms. Morgan said. She touched Dad's shoulder and smiled at him.

"Thank you," Dad said, but right away, he dropped his fork and disappeared under the table to get it.

"I'm going to learn to draw a duck next," I said.

Tyler nodded at me. "A duck will be good, Katie," he said.

Oh no! I thought. Why on earth had I mentioned a duck? Now he would start again on poor baby ducklings looking for their mothers.

But Tyler was sliding his spoon around his plate, chasing a piece of strawberry from the fruit salad. He looked up. "Do a daddy duck. And two little ducks. Just like us."

Dad wiped his fork with a paper napkin and grinned at me. "Whew," he said. He gave me a relieved wink.

Chapter 29

Dad Gets His Call

When we got home from Ms. Morgan's, Dad hurried into the house. "I want to check my voice mail," he said. He went into his office and I heard him dialing. A minute later, he shouted something that I couldn't hear.

It was about the job. I knew it. We were going to have to move.

I looked around our dear family room. The wall by the door had a streak that looked like blue lightning, left from when I tried out my new bike when I was eight. In the backyard, Tyler had a hidey bush. He hid there once for hours while Dad and I looked everywhere for him. A new house wouldn't have our special marks on the walls. It wouldn't have our special places.

"Listen to this." Dad came running out of his office. "I'm turning on the speakerphone so you can hear."

Tyler ran past me to Dad's office.

"I don't want to," I said.

"Come on, Katie," Dad said.

I covered my ears and walked toward my room.

In Dad's office, a voice started to speak.

"Flagstaff here. Bill, old buddy, what's going on? Here I am in Germany, talking to folks in the solar industry. The main company I'm talking to is Solacom. They have offices in Portland. Those guys tell me you want to do projects for them, not me."

I stopped next to Dad's office door.

The voice started again. "I want you to keep working for me. I'll give you a raise. A longer vacation. Anything! Don't . . . tell . . . them . . . yes."

Another pause. "I'll call you Tuesday. Good-bye."

Dad pushed some buttons on the phone and held his finger in the air over the play button.

"He's cut back on the old companies," he said slowly, "because he's more interested in solar energy. That makes perfect sense." He pushed the button. Mr. Flagstaff said everything again.

"That's Mr. Friend talking to us," Tyler said. "I need to get my trucks out so he can play with me." He ran down the hall to his room.

I stood very still. "Does this mean . . . ?" I asked. But my throat closed up. I couldn't say another word.

Dad held his arms out to me. He folded me close and rocked me back and forth. At last, his voice rumbled against my ear. "No Portland. We're staying right here."

I listened to him breathing, slow and deep as the confusions of the whole week began to sort themselves out. No more thinking about whether our house had lines. No more cleaning up my closet and giving things away.

"I should call Janna," Dad said. "Tell her."

I pulled away from him. "Too much is happening. I have to talk to Sierra right this minute."

"She doesn't even know about it," Dad said. "Does she?"

"I have to tell her anyway," I said. "She needs to know we almost lost each other forever!"

At that moment the phone rang. "Why hello!" Dad said. "We were just talking about you." He grinned as he handed me the phone.

"Hi, Katie," Sierra's voice said. "We're standing in a long line at this restaurant Grandma likes. Dad said since I was driving him crazy, I could call you on his cell phone."

"I have to tell you important things," I told her. "Dad and Tyler and I almost had to move to Portland. I wasn't going to see you anymore."

"You can't move away," Sierra yelled, and I heard someone hush her. Her voice got a little softer. "You can't move away. We've got plans! I just talked Mom into letting me ride my bike to your house."

"We're not moving," I told her. "We just found out we're not moving."

I heard Sierra's voice telling her family the news. As she talked to them, I watched Dad, sorting papers on his desk. He threw Real Estate Sadie's card into the wastebasket, and a huge weight lifted out of my stomach. Then, he got the card back out. "Have to let her know," he muttered to me. "Tell her we're not selling."

"My whole family says you cannot move to Portland," Sierra said. "But if you do, you can live with me. Mom said you can have the bedroom with the green stripes."

My eyes filled with happy tears. Sierra was better than a best friend. She was like a sister. "Tell your mom thanks," I said, but then I looked at Dad's face as he sorted through his papers. "But if I lived with you, I would miss Tyler and Dad." I sighed. Things were never simple.

"We went up the Space Needle," Sierra said. "And we went to a market where they throw huge fish around in the air."

"We went to Mom's concert last night," I told her. I took a deep breath and rushed on. "And today, we went to Ms. Morgan's house for a barbecue."

"Oh my gosh! Ms. Morgan's?"

"In her backyard."

"Oopsie, the line is moving," Sierra said. "Dad wants his phone back. I have to say good-bye."

"Good-bye," I said. "See you next week."

As I put down the phone, I hit myself on the head. "I forgot to tell her about Lucy! But Dad! You still haven't said . . ."

Dad touched my arm. "Yes. Lucy will be our dog. I'm sure we'll have her by the time Sierra gets home." He smiled at me. "Any chance I could use the phone now?"

I was still clutching it. "It's sort of hot and wet," I said, handing it to him, "from talking to Sierra."

"I'm going to call Janna," he said.

"And the next question is . . ." I drew in a breath, all at once, scared to even think about Ms. Morgan and Dad.

"Will she . . . ?" I stopped and rubbed my damp hands on my shorts. "Be our new mother?"

He stopped dialing and put the phone down. "Katie," he said. "New mothers take time. Months. Sometimes, years!"

"Years?" I stared at him.

"First, you get to be good friends," Dad said.

"But you really like her, don't you, Dad?"

"She is special," he said. "I was glad to find out that Eric is only her brother." He stood up. "I wonder if I might have my office to myself for this call."

"Years?" I repeated.

"In the meantime, there's the dog," Dad said, whooshing me toward the door.

"The dog!" I rushed out of his office and down the hall to Tyler's room. "Tyler, Tyler, Tyler," I yelled. "We're not moving! We're staying here! We're getting Lucy!"

As Dad closed his office door, Tyler ran into the hall and stared at me with wide, blue eyes.

"Uh-oh," he said as he scooted back into his room and leaped into Lucy's box. "She's going to sleep right here," he yelled. "You can't have her."

"No way, Tyler. We have to share!" I rushed into his room and leaned over him. "That's what families do."

His eyes peeked over the top of the box.

"Okay," he said in a softer voice. "Come in here. Maybe we can all fit."

"It's too crowded." I watched him scoot into one corner. Making room for me.

"Crowded is good, Katie."

Crowded with Tyler. Crowded with Lucy. We would always make room for one more.

I climbed in beside him.

Anne Warren Smith grew up in the Adirondack Mountains of upstate New York. She spends her winters in Tucson, Arizona, and lives the rest of the year in Corvallis, Oregon. For many years she performed folk music in coffee houses and dreamed of becoming a star, but she never got to be as famous as Katie's mom.

Katie's story began with *Turkey Monster Thanksgiving* and continues with *Tails of Spring Break.*

For more about the author, visit www.annewarrensmith.com

Read all three stories about Katie Jordan!